For the ones who believed in me.

THE SMOKER'S SOURCE

Grey Liliy

Published by Broken Pocket in 2015 in The United States of America.

ISBN-13: 978-1943161003
ISBN-10: 1943161003

Cover by Grey Liliy

CHAPTER 1

GUARDS. INMATES. NO difference between them really, save for maybe which side of the bars they happened to be standing on.

Francis let the cigarette linger between his fingertips. The smoke curled in the open air, twisting and climbing through dancing dust particles like an unwanted friend. The rolled paper met his lips, and he inhaled life, exhaling slowly. He savored every bit of the tar, nicotine, and drugs prepackaged into what some people would call a quicker death.

Francis smoked.

Always had, and he always would, thanks to a certain guard catering to his habit. Francis learned early on in this decrepit place that the Warden didn't care what you had, or how you got it, as long as it wasn't a flat out weapon. That was the line, and most folks weren't too keen on crossing it. Francis shook the pack of off-brand nicotine dressed in white, and counted the three sticks left. He wondered if his source had managed to sneak another pack in yet, or if he'd have to start rationing.

Not that he could be blamed for blowing through his stash so quickly when there was a new guard in town. It was the sort of new blood that made everyone nervous, or in some cases excited. Either way, it made excellent rational to justify his increased chain smoking. Francis tapped his cigarette against his ash tray. The newest guy roaming their block, now he was a nasty piece of work—which is saying something from a guy who slit throats for a living. Only Tobias Memorial could churn out guards like that, and still somehow uphold the falsified reputation as "safe and secure housing for dangerous felons" in the outside world.

But it was home, one way or another.

His Tobias Memorial Prison was a cozy little penitentiary that took up the entirety of a small man-made island just off the coast of Virginia. Built in 1923, it was a veritable fortress of steel, wire, darkness, and a surprisingly well kept rose garden courtesy of the B-Block. The pansies over in B had pooled together to negotiate with the guards for the privilege of tending the center courtyard as they pleased, and they went with roses. Francis didn't particularly care to know what was exchanged in the bargain, but he did realize B-Block felt it was worth their dignity, pride, or whatever else they gave up for the right to play in the dirt.

Francis figured they were all nuts bending over backwards to the guards' demands. Then again, they loved those stupid flowers more than their dignity. B-Block covered their cells in clippings of the things until the rotting petals dried between borrowed library books and littered their floor in a sea of brown. Francis would take his smokes any day, just like every other self respecting member of good ol' G-Block. He scooted up on his cot to place his back against the cool wall, sucking a drag of smoke into his lungs. Francis couldn't say too much about B-Block, though. Heaven knows he'd probably go to the same lengths or further to keep his cigarettes coming…

The guards though, they weren't exactly the type you wanted to be owing favors. They were every bit as rotten as the inmates, but smarter. They'd be behind bars before you could stub out a cigarette butt in some stool-pigeon's arm if they had ever actually been caught in action. Francis flicked a dime's worth of ash into the black tray sitting on the edge of his pristine, rock-hard, mattress. All of them were potential cellmates, trapped just like the rest behind the chipped, rotten brickwork of the prison. Francis sucked in a swig of smoke. J-Block's head guard, for example, had personally done hits for the local mob—gruesome stuff that made Francis itch under his skin just hearing the offhand details. That fella made quite a living doing that up until he got bored and wanted something more 'stable.'

The rest of the staff wasn't much better.

Such as the aforementioned new guy of G-Block. Francis had yet to pin down just what was knocked loose in that guy's head, and it rattled in his brain like a loose gear. The new guard was a shrimp of a man, yet somehow still lanky with limbs too long for his torso. He had slicked red hair, beady brown eyes, and an appetite that sickened even the hardest man's stomach. Guy'd bitten a finger off some poor sap at the opposite end of Francis' row who just couldn't keep it to himself, pointing and waving his hand through the steel open bars. Guard was a quick thing; moved before you realized you'd set him off. The guard giggled like a hyena, too, watching like a scavenger waiting for his chance to steal a strip of flesh from the big cats.

Francis considered himself lucky he still had three cigarettes left with how his heart pounded every time Guard Liam Hurst walked by the gate, baton in hand. Oh, what he wouldn't give for a go at—

"You're going to make yourself sick if you keep smoking so many of those in a row," a soothing tenor said through the iron bars of Francis' cell.

"Then maybe you should stop giving them to me." Francis crooked the side of his mouth into a smirk, smothering the remainder of his cigarette in the tray alongside his daydreams of digging a blade through Hyena Hurst's throat.

There was always an exception to every rule—much to Francis' good fortune—and when it came to Tobias Memorial Prison, his name was Ollie Blake.

Ollie had eyes as green as his namesake, warm tan skin, a classically handsome face, and smooth dirty brown hair that fell in a slight wave to the top of his ears. Together, these features made up the young guard who'd taken an awful liking to Francis E. Hackney. The kid was ten years his junior at an energetic twenty-two, and was too friendly for his own good. Probably would have been killed years ago if not for a few good eyes watching his back like a hawk. Ollie'd joined the prison staff for personal reasons that had yet to be plucked from his person by staff or inmate alike, but Francis guessed it was some sort of misguided good will.

Ollie's uniform was as freshly pressed as the day he got it. The creases in the old-fashioned black uniform suit were as crisp as a freshly split apple. Guard uniforms were complete with suit jacket, black tie, and a belt over the jacket holding their equipment. To keep the inmates in line, guards carried a pistol, a baton, a flashlight, and a small pouch full of whatever baubles and trinkets they needed to bribe the inmates. Usually things any other penitentiary would choke upon learning their inmates had.

What most prisons would consider hazards, Tobias Memorial appreciated as civilized. It was the same logic that had guards carrying loaded pistols within hand-reach of inmates, Francis guessed. But, then again, most folks weren't stupid enough to attack a wild dog, and the ones that were—well. Francis remembered what happened to the one poor soul who thought he had it covered, but there was no sense in getting himself worked up with Ollie standing two feet away, all youth and Hollywood handsome in his uniform.

It almost made him feel self-conscious.

Francis was the kid's opposite. Next to Ollie, he felt old with premature wrinkles around the edges of his eyes. Francis was tall and broad though, standing a good foot and a half over the kid. He was sinewy muscle and grace craved by years of work and upkeep, wrapped in a button down shirt, slacks, and slip-on shoes. With dirty blonde hair and hazel eyes, Francis wasn't as handsome as Ollie, but he wasn't ugly either. His Ma, rest in peace, used to call him 'rugged' once upon a time.

Francis looked like his dad, he supposed, but after slicing the artery in your old man's neck, you tended to stop caring about family resemblance.

Francis didn't know why the kid liked him so much, but if Ollie kept bringing him cigarettes for the low, low price of company, Francis would humor him all day and night. "Sick? What's to worry there, Ollie? It's not like I have anywhere to be, and who knows? It might shorten my sentence."

"You shouldn't talk like that," Ollie said, his face disappointed, but his eyes smiling. He tapped the edge of the bar with the tip of his baton, light and playful. Francis closed the box top on his cigarettes and tossed them on the mattress. Ollie grinned just enough to hint at white, straight teeth. "Then who'll I talk to on rounds?"

"Johnson?" Francis asked, tilting his head toward the dark-headed guard smacking the bars on the other side of the room. While somehow still maintaining an air of boredom, Johnson kicked the bottom of the irons, shouting random obscenities between his orders of *go to sleep*. Francis shrugged, and licked the edge of his lip. "He is your partner."

"I can talk to Johnson any time," Ollie said. His face dropped, overcome by something more serene and contemplative than his usual demeanor. Like he was trying to hide the unusual frown, Ollie perked up into a sudden smile. "Besides, he can get grumpy when he's working. Not nearly as up for friendly conversation this hour as you are."

"Isn't it your bedtime, Ollie?" Francis asked, scratching his scalp through blonde hair. Ollie's estranged partner was one thing, but the kid leant on the bars like he was waiting for a date instead of doing a routine bed check like he always did. Some days Francis wondered what would happen if Ollie got bored and doted on some other inmate instead of his favorite smoker. Francis shifted on the bed to face the bars, hands on his knees as he leaned over. He'd probably have fewer cigarettes—and be locked in solitary for snapping his competitor's neck. "Brats like you should be asleep when the sun goes down."

"Not for another three hours, and you know it." Ollie shook his head, amused by Francis' banter. He placed his arm up on the bars over his head, blocking the rest of the room, nestling the two of them in an illusion of privacy. The kid had no sense of self-preservation, and Francis loved it. Ollie smiled in that pleasant way of his, eyes open and honest as he continued lightly tapping the baton on the bars. Teasing Francis. Ollie pressed his lips together, and shrugged just enough to crinkle the fabric of his jacket. "Plenty of time to visit."

"And you know how I love the company," Francis said, only half of it sarcasm. He played nice for the smokes, true, but he'd probably have done so either way. Ollie Blake was what was known as a 'genuinely good person' to the rest of the world. Kind, smart as a tack, and full of that good old Christian brotherly love—the real, genuine article. Kid cared about everyone, even the killers, the murderers, and the thieves, like his Good Book told him to.

It'd get Ollie killed sooner or later, but for now Francis would enjoy someone who didn't know any better than to stay away from the dangerous folk. Someone who treated Francis like he was human; an addiction worse than his nicotine. Francis leaned toward the bars, grinning like the devil. "You're something else, you know that kid?"

"W-would you two lovebirds knock it off?" Coal said from the adjoining cell, snug between Francis and an empty nook of a hallway.

Coal's hands clamped around the bars, with his face pressed between them. A defensive snarl showed off his yellowed teeth, and his raven black hair spiked in wild directions. Coal's brown eyes were open wide, pupils constantly dilated for reasons Francis guessed cost him a pretty penny. The undersides of those beady dots were plagued by dark bags against his tan skin. Those, he knew, were caused by the insomnia. Stubble rubbed against the metal, probably irritating his chin if the way he reached up to scratch the side of his cheek was any indication.

Iron bars and familiarity were his bravery. Otherwise Coal'd be a shivering wreck unable to shout at a bug, let alone Ollie. "I'm trying to watch my stories!"

The stories in your head, you mean. Francis pushed back on his bunk, letting his head hit the wall. Coal was the nuttiest of the nutty. His head was a TV stuck on daytime repeat, but with only one show on the air. Coal'd recite the dialog out loud once in a while, and it wasn't uncommon for an inmate or two to listen in. A few even kept up with the plot. Ollie had offered Coal pens and paper once to write his stories down once, but the loony-bin reject hissed at the utensils. He claimed it would violate the sacred nature of his stories. How he'd ended up in quiet little G-Block was an even bigger mystery than how Ollie became a guard in this dump.

"I'm sorry, Mr. Coal. We'll try and be quiet." Ollie rubbed the back of his head sheepishly, in what was likely actual guilt. His tone was sincere, and made Francis' stomach churn in an odd way that was probably related to a green-eyed monster or two.

He hated sharing his things.

"Nonsense," a new voice interrupted. Francis shivered in delight at the dulcet tone, more scared and excited of the voice's owner than hyena-boy any day. If he were a man of lesser control, Francis would have gotten on his knees and crawled to the bars to get a closer look. Instead he closed his eyes and listened to Guard Emmanuel Shepherd speak. It was a low, soothing voice—cold, and black as night itself. A voice that promised death to the fullest. "You're a guard, Oliver: he should do what you say, and keep his mouth shut otherwise."

"He's not hurting anything, Em," Ollie said, turning away from the prisoners' cells to address the head of G-Block.

Francis licked his lips hearing the nickname fall from the young man's lips. Shepherd was Ollie's superior, and had insisted from day one that the young man use the abbreviation. None of the other guards were extended the same privilege. Shepherd used and expected the use of full names and titles when addressing your superiors in all other circumstances.

Shepherd was worse about his favoritism than Ollie.

"It can't hurt to humor him just a little," Ollie said, pinching his forefinger and thumb together. He clipped his baton back onto his belt, and smoothed his jacket down. The boy stood up an inch straighter, and adjusted his tie to match with the enthusiasm of a puppy. Francis flicked his pack of cigarettes. "It's good for them to know we listen."

"You give an inch, they take a mile. You know that." Shepherd dropped his pale hand on the boy's shoulder and squeezed. Francis

10

wanted to cut it off at the wrist. Shepherd faked sincerity like a champ as he cooed at Ollie. "I worry for you. One of these days they're going to take advantage of you, and then what?"

Francis kept quiet, and watched a master at work. Shepherd the predator. Pale skin that would have made Snow White jealous, stretched thin around a muscular frame. The man was about the same age as Francis, and shared the same blond hair, only neater kept. Francis could never quite manage the combed, slick side part. Shepherd had eyes the color of coal; an endless pupil in the flash of white. He looked perpetually, deceptively sick which was quite the natural defense against the unaware. A serial killer head to toe, everything about Shepherd was built to decimate the living. Francis would bet his life on it.

It was easy to recognize your own kind.

Shepherd was also fond as hell of the prison's own little good boy, Ollie Blake. He was Shepherd's chosen pup of the pack, and the head guard spoiled him as rotten as a grandma would her grand-baby. It made Francis' skin crawl, but he was smart enough to keep his mouth shut around the trigger happy guard. Besides, if Shepherd hadn't claimed dibs on the kid, Francis had a feeling little Ollie would have been bent over a few surfaces against his will a hundred times over by now. If not that, he'd be sporting daily new bruises like they were going out of fashion. Everyone loved a good boy. Francis sneered at the wall when Ollie smiled up at his buddy 'Em.'

"You worry too much. I can handle Coal and Hackney." Ollie patted the hand still clenching his shoulder twice before holding on and squeezing. Shepherd smiled at the contact. Francis plucked his box from the bed and held it in his lap. Ollie released Shepherd's hand, and rubbed his forehead under the brim of his hat with the back of his thumb. "Looks like my visit is over though. If you're here, it means I'm a tad behind bed checks."

"Good lad," Shepherd said. He pushed Ollie forward by the back shoulder. "Get going then. Off with you."

A moment of silence passed as the older guard kept his gaze firmly on Ollie as he passed each cell, granting each occupant a nod of the head and a 'good night.' Francis felt the temperature drop, when Shepherd's eyes narrowed. They focused on Francis without having to turn his head. Francis wasn't the only one who didn't like to share. "You really should learn not to fraternize with the guards, naive as they may be."

The man had spoken in plurals, but they both knew there was only one guard Francis held conversation with. Francis kept Shepherd framed in the corner of his eye, but spoke to the bare wall in front of him. "Can't help it if it's rude to not reply to the little chatterbox."

"We'll see," Shepherd said in a voice laced with warning. Francis squirmed on his rock of a mattress; in the good way. He had visions of spilt blood, burning flesh and wax. Shepherd's black eyes reflected his thoughts with equal venom. "Take care, Hackney."

Francis popped another cigarette into his mouth. Two left.

CHAPTER 2

OLIVER HUNG HIS hat on the hook in his dented locker. He un-clipped his security belt and placed it below, the rusted hook rattling under the weight. Oliver's gun followed, locked safely in its carrying case, and he stowed his flashlight neatly on the top shelf between a small Bible and a box of cherry candies. The locker room was dim, lit mostly by the flickering of the overhead light, and Oliver's nose twitched as a light breeze carried the damp smell of mold from the showers next door. Outside the window, the security lighting stopped a foot from the building, a gradient of pale light to pitch black in two steps. It was like an inky soup, and his walk home was sure to be smothering as always.

Oliver undid the straps of his heavy bullet-proof vest, and slid it off his shoulders to throw in the bottom of the locker. He didn't envy the folks who had to keep up with the night shift. It was as lonely and dark in the prison over night as it was outside. And of course there was the unofficial no-talking rule. The inmates liked their sleep, and got agitated by chatty guards in the middle of the night trying to stay awake in the depressing atmosphere. Oliver didn't think conversations with Francis would be nearly as satisfying if one of them was asleep.

Oliver felt a tap on his shoulder.

"You owe me," Johnson said, starting the conversation cold. He tossed a carton of cigarettes at Oliver, caught after a slight fumble. Johnson snorted, and scratched the back of his head after a yawn. His partner's black hair was as messy as Coal's, and similar ever-present bags under his eyes hung above his cheeks like coats on a rack. Johnson's usually warm mulch-color eyes looked faded and glossy tonight, far more than usual. Johnson loosened his tie, and dropped onto the locker next to

13

Oliver's with a thud. He leant against it, rubbing under his nose. "Next time you can't make a boat trip to the mainland, tell your boy-toy he can suffer without them for a week or two."

"I will be sure to do that, however, I do still appreciate it this time." Oliver dropped the carton in the bottom of his locker, ignoring the insult to Francis.

Johnson complained, but he'd only had to do it twice. The jail chaplain only needed help with Communion twice a year. They really needed to add a few more trips to the boat roster, or at least move the trip to Saturday instead of Sunday. The sea Captain would probably appreciate a doubled schedule as well. He always said ferrying the guards was more entertaining than carrying tourists back and forth on the main land.

Oliver shut his locker, and clicked the lock into place. "Did I give you enough?"

"Ah, that's right. You gave me too much, actually," Johnson said, scrunching his nose up at the thought. He reached into his back pocket and flipped through a few bills before dropping a ten in Oliver's hand. "There was a sale or something."

"Thanks," Oliver said. He stuffed the bill in his pocket. The room was quiet with the shuffle, and Johnson didn't look like he was moving any time soon. Oliver cleared his throat. "How's your model air craft carrier coming? You mentioned something about getting parts for it."

"Pretty good," Johnson said, shuffling in on himself. For a moment, he looked like Francis slouched on his bed in the cell, only without the constant air of confidence. Johnson was oddly shy for a man who Oliver had seen body slam a fleeing inmate. Johnson straightened with a tiny smile after a moment. "Finally found a paint color I liked. Gunmetal grey."

Oliver grinned, patting Johnson on the shoulder in congratulations. "That's great. You'll have to show me when it's done."

"Maybe." Johnson shifted, rubbing his shoulder into a dent in the locker. "Might be for a while, though. Won't have time to paint it until next week."

"Yeah, we're all so busy it's hard to find the time for hobbies." Oliver said. He pat Johnson on the shoulder one last time, before heading for the locker room door. He turned and walked backwards as he said his goodbyes. "So, I guess I'll see you for tomorrow's shift."

"Like everyday," Johnson said, yawning into his hand and pushing off

14

the lockers.

Oliver drummed his fingers on the metal locker room door, unsure if he should say anything more before leaving the room. Conversations that flowed so smoothly with Francis turned to awkward silence with his partner almost without fail. It shouldn't be so hard! Oliver forced his posture to perk up. "Thanks again for picking up the cigarettes!"

"Yeah, yeah. I hope whatever Hackney is givin' up for those things is worth it to you." Johnson shook his head and headed off toward the showers. "It's an expensive little habit he's got."

Oliver paused at the door, his hand on the knob. He tilted his head, listening for Johnson's footsteps to disappear. He smiled softly to himself, thinking of Francis flipping open a new package. Chewing on the edge of the little white stick with chapped lips wrapped around it. Oliver turned the door handle, pushing it open with a loud creak. "It's worth it."

CHAPTER 3

FRANCIS HELD HIS hand over his eyes, blocking out the sun pounding down on the prison yard. The crisp and cool weather of Fall brought a new sort of desolation to their grey rock. Any hint of green was hidden away behind the brick and mortar of the main jailhouse in a tiny courtyard controlled by B-Block. The guards and their families had a few grass fields to use on the opposite side of the island, but it was blocked from the inmate's view by the main building and a paved road.

The inmates' 'yard' was nothing more than a concrete patch in the corner of the island. Two sides of the square were flush against the prison building, with steep concrete stairs climbing mid-way up the block wall. The the rest of the yard was penned in by standard chain-link fences that looked out over the ocean. They didn't bother with the razor wire along the top, though. If you survived the forty-foot fall to the sharp rocks below, you deserved an attempt to swim to shore.

The Warden knew where to save money.

The prison was divided into ten blocks, each bedding down twenty cells with one inmate per. Fifteen guards were assigned to each block working in pairs, with the odd-numbered head guard overseeing as he felt fit. Each block shared a schedule, which meant you played together, ate together, and worked together. Francis found it rather cozy. Team-building and cliques, and all that.

Yard time was the big exception, during which all ten blocks were let out to play at the same time. Tobias Memorial was practically a high school. The inmates kept to their own cliques as they huddled in corners talking, or playing the occasional game like teenagers. Francis scratched the side of his hair, and cracked his spine on the step as he stretched.

Inmates were assigned their block based on personality, more so than the level of their crimes, so it worked out for the best. It was amazing how well a serial killer and a car-thief could get along once they discovered a mutual love of gardening.

Blocks E, F, and G were home to the 'normal' inmates—otherwise known as the baddies who could pass for your every day John Doe. They liked quiet, and being treated like adults. Sure, the occasional oddity slipped through the cracks, like Francis' oh so delightful neighbor Coal, but for the most part they were civilized enough. Ollie once said that E, F, and G were the most dangerous felons in the building, "Because their image didn't seem to fit their crimes."

Francis didn't disagree. Ollie's precious "Em" would be in the same cell block if he was ever locked up.

Now if only yard time could manage to stop being so boring, Francis thought to himself for not the first time. You'd think more would go on with an entire yard full of inmate ticking time bombs inches away from each other.

But no, everyone kept to their usual activities, day in and day out. Made for boring people watching, that was for sure.

Francis spotted a couple arranging flowers in a corner sticking white and red roses in a vase they had made during arts and crafts. Definitely inmates from B-Block. One was even trimming the excess leaves off the edges of the plant. Artwork for no one but each other. Francis tapped a cigarette on the step edge, kicking the ash off to blend into the grey steps. Blocks A and B were for the peculiars with obsessive-compulsive issues— see B and their plants for example. Block A just liked things clean. Spotless, sterile and unnatural.

Francis flexed his fingers. C and D were for the screamers, no further explanation necessary. Crazy Hyena Hurst would either be there if he were ever convicted, or stuck with H, I and J were homes to the violent lots. The criminals with big mouths and something to prove were gathered there to feed off each other's egos and tempers. It was hard to tell which fit him best, but Hyena Hurst still somehow ended up a guard in good old G-Block with Ollie and Shepherd.

He must have requested the position. Francis slid down into the step, scratching an itch on his back. Or maybe he blew Shepherd one day during break and got a transfer.

Hard to tell around this place.

Contemplating guard-inmate relations and bribes only quelled boredom for so long. Francis never was one for the gossip pool. He'd much rather see it in action than hear about it later.

Francis crossed his legs at the ankles, watching some big thug named Bob or Rob shove some loon from C-Block in the shoulder for shouting during lunch. A big hunk of muscle leaning over the poor crazy and shouting bloody murder at the top of his lungs. Francis rubbed between his eyes. Different day, same show. But wasn't that prison in the first place? He shifted when he heard a shout coming from the other end nearest the water. Now that was more like it when it came to yard entertainment. Francis clicked his tongue on the back of his teeth, grinning.

A bulky J-Block guy screamed at one of the saps from B-Block and his rose vase. Francis guessed the big son of a bitch must not like flowers. The tiny gardener whimpered, clutching his flowers to his chest as the larger man towered over him. A small crowd gathered around the two, gaping and peaking over shoulders. B-Block's own scrambled as far away from the behemoth as he could, but didn't get far. J-Block grabbed the back of flower-boy's shirt, and slammed B-Block's head into the nearest step.

Francis jumped to his feet, eyes locked on the splatter of blood sprayed against the surrounding concrete. The smaller man's head was indented against the corner edge, eyes open and unseeing. A halo of red circled the wound, leaving a glorious splash of color against the dull, everyday grey. Francis licked his lips, his pulse racing at the sight of that beautiful red.

Francis loved killing people.

Arterial spray was in the air. It was impossible not to get excited, not to have his skin crawl and beg for more excitement. The iron scent and warmth pulsing out of the limp body awakened his entire being in a sea of adrenaline and hormones. Before his incarceration six years ago, Francis lived for that and nothing else. Women, men, money, and power —none of that mattered as much as the intimate nature of cradling someone's throat near your own, splitting it open as easy as dipping a hot knife into margarine.

Francis' mother never did believe in owning butter.

He was two steps closer to the warm spatter when a hand grabbed his arm. Ollie appeared in the center of his vision. Olive green replaced the brilliant red as the kid forced Francis to make eye contact. The kid squeezed his arm through the coarse cotton fabric, fingers digging in hard enough to feel his nails. "Hackney, keep it together and back away."

Hackney.

Ollie only pulled out the last name when he played at guard instead of his favorite inmate's bosom buddy. The change in tone, and rarity of the event, was enough to cool his blood lust down to a mere twitching arousal. Ollie stood over him, something warm in his eyes—relief, likely. Johnson hovered behind Ollie, his hand on his nightstick looking equally disappointed to Ollie's relief. Francis reached for his cigarette pack and took a seat on the stairs. He had forgotten where he was. Running to the scene was a guaranteed way to give a lesser guard like Ollie's little partner an excuse to lay into you.

The J-Block attacker would be lucky if he got away with a beating and a week or two in solitary.

"Stay here," Ollie warned, squeezing Francis' shoulder. As shouts began to rise from the scene of the murder, Ollie reached for his radio and pressed the 'talk' button. Francis stuck a white stick of nicotine in his mouth as the boy prattled into the hissing static. "This is Guard Blake in the yard. An inmate is down and the crowd is getting riled. Send more back up."

Francis sucked on the unlit cigarette watching Ollie head down the stairs toward the bully and his kill. Johnson followed, weapon brandished and already hitting back at any onlookers who tried to follow along. The inmates and guards crowded around the bloodied spot shoving and yelling. Ollie blended in with the rest of the suits as he went to work, his partner tagging along behind. The kid screamed for folks to back up, pushing his way through cheering bodies and people vomiting as effectively as the rest.

Francis flicked the top flap of his cigarette box.

"That boy's going to get himself killed one of these days," Lyle Chaplin said, tapping Francis in the shoulder with the tip of his toe. "It's like he doesn't have a pinch of self preservation."

Chaplin crossed his arms as he walked down the steps until he was almost head-to-head with Francis. His eyes were wary as he looked over the commotion in the lower yard, but still with a sense of reservation. Chaplin had came in on the same bus as Francis six years ago, and

19

experience had taught how quickly something like a yard fight could spiral out of control.

Chaplin's eyes followed Ollie as he shoved his way through rowdy inmates. "Always jumping in to be the hero."

"Not disagreeing with you." Francis removed the cigarette and rolled it between his fingers. Chaplin, who had resided two cells down from Francis since day one, was a man after his own heart. Six foot four, built like a pro wrestler, and bald as a cue ball, Chaplin was also soft spoken, enjoyed light jazz, and was stuck at Tobias Memorial for the armed robberies of eighteen high profile banks and another twenty mid-level jobs. In total, the guy got away with forty million in cash, and another two million in goods. He had killed four security guards throughout his entire thieving campaign, and regretted each and every one. The gentle giant who could break you in two if you got between him and his take regretted hurting folks—that was Lyle Chaplin.

Behind him, cowering in his britches like a two-year-old at a mall full of clowns, was little Vernon Coal. Francis couldn't even picture finding one without the other these days. Coal had moved in four years ago and a set was made the second they saw each other. Francis thought it was precious, and mutual to boot. Chaplin was Coal's favorite inmate, and the only one who didn't tease the poor, crazy bastard.

"How's your stories, Vern?" Francis asked, distracting himself from the young guard in the middle of the scuffle at the base of the stairs. He couldn't give two shits about Coal's stories, but if it kept him from thinking about that inmate that just elbowed Ollie in the gut, he'd ask. Francis gripped his cigarette hard enough to bend the stick. He itched to jump into the fight and make a few blood splatters of his own. "Julie and Max get together yet?"

"N-no," Coal answered, his voice muffled through the thick fabric of their standard-issue jacket collar he had pulled up over his muzzle. "She's still flirting with Jack."

"Isn't that just like her? Her perfect man is standing right there, and she doesn't even turn to him," Chaplin said with a shake of the head. Unlike Francis, he kept up to date on the latest episodes every lunch block when Coal gave his daily event rundown. "You'd think she'd notice Jack isn't any good for her."

The sound of flesh meeting flesh echoed out from the side, and Francis dared to look over as the other two chatted about fictional soap operas.

The big J-Block oaf who'd started the whole mess was laid flat on the ground, still as the man he'd cracked open. Shepherd stood over the body, delicately rubbing the knuckles of his right hand.

Francis regretted looking away.

The yard was silent, and not a single sign of a riot remained in the statue-like gawkers. The inmates and guards had formed a scattered circle around Shepherd, the body, and Ollie at his side in their panic to get away from the eye of the storm. A black uniformed guard was speckled here or there in the sea of pale button downs, looked as equally intimidated as the men under their care. Shepherd was the ring master of this little circus, standing tall, proud, and deadly. The closest onlooker was twenty feet away with a look of horror etched on their face, but Ollie looked impressed with whatever it was Shepherd had done. He stood at his side, saying something with a smile.

Francis stood up from his seat, looking over everything from his place on the steps. Shepherd wrapped an arm around Ollie's shoulder and walked him to the building's door without so much as a backwards glance to the behemoth he'd taken down. The circle of inmates parted for the two of them like the sea did for Moses. Francis scoffed at his own metaphor. He'd been listening to Ollie too much when he pestered him for missing Chapel on Sunday afternoons. The inmates and guards kept their eyes on Shepherd and his charge until the door closed behind them. Even Johnson lingered behind, shoulders hunched and unsure. Shepherd's grimy fingers kept their place on Ollie every step of the way.

After a beat, a few guards scuffled out of the circle to the center of the storm. Clean up. The inmates backed away to their respective parts of the yard and their chatty little cliques as the guards restrained the bully in a pair of thick cuffs. One threw a sheet over the dead man until the Doc could come pick him up. The circle disintegrated, Shepherd was gone, and just like that, life was back to its usual in the yard.

"I don't like that man," Coal hissed from behind Chaplin's leg. Francis figured he wasn't talking about Ollie or the bully for J-Block. Coal's hands trembled as he clutched Chaplin's jacket. "He's scary."

"You said it." Francis stuffed his unlit cigarette back in the box.

CHAPTER 4

GUARD EMMANUEL SHEPHERD. *Guard* Emmanuel Shepherd.

He'd always loved the way that sounded. Emmanuel sipped coffee from his pristine bone china tea cup, the pattern briar rose. Life was about elegance and brutality meeting at a crossroad and uniting as one. It was absolute.

Across from him, Guard Oliver Blake fumbled with his drink, unsure of how to grip the delicate handle of the cup. The boy gave up a moment later, as he always did, and held the cup by its base with his fingers wrapped under and through the handle, like one would hold a common coffee mug. Emmanuel let it pass.

It was nothing but rudeness to openly correct such a welcome guest.

Besides, if Guard Oliver Blake hadn't learned to hold a teacup properly by now, it was doubtful he'd ever get it right. Emmanuel was lucky that the uncultured part of Guard Oliver Blake's being only added to the boy's charm. Like raising a child, the boy's attempts at adulthood were more endearing than cumbersome. He brought a much needed warm body into Emmanuel's lonesome quarters.

The guards lived in a row of townhouses on the east side of the island. Each unit had room for a guard and his family, though most chose to live alone or with a single roommate. Emmanuel could only name three or four guards that he knew personally who had chosen to live with their loved ones, though he was sure there were more. The pitter patter of tiny feet could be heard playing in the front yard every so often in the evenings, or dashing about down the hill in the soccer field they fought so hard to gain permission to build. While a living quarter, kitchenette, and two bedrooms was tight for a family of four, it was ample space for a bachelor like Emmanuel, or his little Guard Oliver Blake.

Emmanuel's home was spartan, but with class. Everything neatly kept, and decorated just enough to keep it from being considered philistine. A china cabinet was the centerpiece of the living area, filled with usable dish ware. The vast mixture of patterns and styles created a diverse beauty whose aesthetic charm was accented only by their utilitarian purpose. What was the point of displaying such things if you didn't use them? The cabinet itself was made from cherry-colored wood that matched his chairs and stout center table. A vase sat in the middle full of fresh cut roses, as they were the only thing the inmates would grow.

Not that he minded. Roses were his own favorite flower as well.

Emmanuel and Guard Oliver Blake each chose to live alone, but that didn't mean they were above socializing. Emmanuel insisted his dear charge join him for tea at least once a week, and supper twice. They took turns cooking on those nights—Emmanuel roasts and lamb, while Guard Oliver Blake often brought stew or macaroni and cheese. Guard Oliver Blake always offered to help clean afterwards, whether he cooked or not. Emmanuel appreciated the gesture every time.

Guard Oliver Blake was a good boy that way.

"Is that a new painting, Em?" Guard Oliver Blake asked around a sip of black coffee. Shepherd didn't believe in ruining good coffee or tea with such extras as sugar and cream. Extravagance and class were not one and the same, and Emmanuel bought excellent coffee. Guard Oliver Blake put the cup back down on the table, slowly as to not chip the saucer. "I don't remember seeing it before."

The portrait in question hung vertically above the small gas fireplace from the ceiling down to an inch above the mantel shelf: A lady nestled in the grass of a field, nude save for a blanket of wild flowers. She slept on with open eyes, her hands crossed over her waist in serene peace. Blonde hair cascaded over her breasts and intermingled with the dappled green grass, highlighted by multi-colored flower petals. Her eyes were dead and empty. A soul-sucking crystal blue behind half-lidded eyes.

Emmanuel found it at an art gallery last week, its artist as six feet under as the subject of his art. While the canvas piece was lovely, the artist's blood that had painted the walls was a far more enchanting shade of red than acrylics could ever capture. *How thoughtful of Guard Oliver Blake to notice the addition.* Emmanuel smiled over his teacup, remembering the screams and cracking bones that accompanied its acquisition.

The painting had been an afterthought, much like most of his china collection.

"Yes, do you like it?" Emmanuel asked, taking a sip of his coffee.

"It's very beautiful, despite the subject," Guard Oliver Blake said. He picked his drink back up, and spun the cup around in his fingers. He tilted his head, his eyes glancing around the room at Emmanuel's collection. Guard Oliver Blake tapped his finger on a daffodil painted on the side of his cup, making eye contact with Emmanuel. He spoke directly. "I think it suits you."

Satisfied with the answer, Emmanuel finished his coffee in the comfortable silence that followed. The artfully crafted cuckoo clock on the wall chimed eight a few moments later, and he set his cup on the table. "As much as I love your visits, Oliver, I do believe it's time to prepare for my night shift."

"Of course," Guard Oliver Blake stood, replacing his cup on its saucer. Black liquid sloshed in the bottom, lightly coating the sides of the porcelain. Poor Guard Oliver Blake had no taste for the finer things. He knew as much about good coffee as he did which was the proper fork to use at a ten course meal. At least he was a good boy. Guard Oliver Blake wiped his hand on his shirt, and pat the back of his chair. "I'll see you tomorrow, Em."

"Have a good night, Oliver." Emmanuel showed him to the door, his hand resting lightly on the boy's arm. He stopped Guard Oliver Blake before he could leave, an afterthought striking him. "Don't forget to clean the present I gave you a few weeks ago. I know it's tucked away for emergency use only, but upkeep is still important."

"I won't forget, Em. Thanks again for thinking of me, too." Guard Oliver Blake slapped the side of Emmanuel's arm. The rough gesture spoke of his time spent with the inmates. Emmanuel really must do something before more of their crude behavior rubbed off on the impressionable boy. Guard Oliver Blake snapped his fingers, grinning widely. "Oh, before I forget!"

"Yes, Oliver?" Emmanuel said, smiling. "What is it?"

"The captain invited me to see his granddaughter when she pulled into port this weekend. She's going fishing, and wants some help carrying her catch." Guard Oliver Blake flexed his arm, holding it up even with his shoulder. "Care to join us?"

"That's alright," Emmanuel said. He shook his head. Leaving the main center of the island would be too far from the inmates. How could he do his job from the water? It was kind to offer, though. "I really wouldn't want to be a bother, so I'll have to decline."

"You wouldn't be, but if you change your mind let me know." Guard Oliver Blake waved, as he tapped down the stairs and onto the grey-stone street. Emmanuel watched him travel the four houses down to his own empty home. The boy waved cheerfully one more time before passing his threshold. Emmanuel shut the door with a silent click. He took a breath, and proceeded to put away his tea cups and kettle.

Such a good boy.

CHAPTER 5

LYLE PULLED THE warm clothes out of the dryer and tossed them on the growing pile in the beige hand cart. Laundry wasn't his first choice for work assignments, but it was better than scrubbing floors or toilets. He grabbed the cart's handle and dragged the bulky basket over to the folding table, taking his usual place by Vernon. The little man was almost done with his first stack, working steadily. Vernon's work was neater than his shaking hands should be able, but there the shirts sat all the same: neat and tightly folded. Lyle pat the small man on the head, ruffling Vernon's wiry hair, and started on his own set of shirts.

Five minutes of folding later, and Lyle stopped working. He put his hands on the table, his fingers gripping the coarse fabric beneath. Vernon folded quietly beside him, mumbling to himself as usual, but there was something that tugged in his stomach. Something wrong. Lyle inhaled deeply, and noted the fresh smell of linens and fabric soap. That was it— he couldn't smell smoke. Lyle picked up the dropped shirt and returned to his work, glancing around the room for the third member of their little clique who wore an ashy scent like a second skin. Lyle exhaled heavily when he spotted the man, his fingers curling into stiff fabric.

Francis had nestled up cozy with Blake in the far corner of the laundry room. The guard's partner Johnson was across on the other side near the main door, flipping a pocket knife open and shut, more or less ignoring his smaller partner's deviance. *Nothing new there,* Lyle sighed. But Blake and Francis weren't just talking, it looked like. His addict buddy must be refreshing his stocks from his favorite source, and Lyle confirmed it when a flash of white packaging showed up.

From Blake's side pack to Francis' pocket, a package of cigarettes disappeared seamlessly in a practiced routine. Blake never failed to deliver, and Francis was never without the stale smell of aged smoke lingering on his clothes and hair. For someone who was supposedly a Bible-thumper, you'd think sneaking inmates 'contraband' would be against Blake's principles. Then again, his more devious actions were usually reserved for a certain smoker, and only that certain smoker.

Blake was kind to everyone, but he was *obsessed* with Francis.

Lyle knew it went both ways, too, whether Francis cared to admit it or not. The man acted differently around the kid—more talkative, and more smiles, as crooked as they were. He denied it, of course, but you'd have to be blind not to see how the man watched Blake when he was around, or how his teeth started to show through a snarl when Shepherd was babying his favorite. It made Lyle wonder if Francis was actually getting his cigarettes for free like he claimed. Favors weren't unheard of for goods, just ask B-Block some day. Keep it up long enough, and some sort of connection was bound to grow, same as the roses in the center yard.

Lyle snorted and kept folding his clothes.

"You think Hackney has a thing for that guard?" Vernon asked, peering up at Lyle from behind his stack of clothes. He sniffed, rubbing his nose with the edge of his cuffed sleeve. The trembling man glanced between Francis and Lyle in quick, tiny jerks, looking like a mouse checking for cats around the corner. "They're always talking."

"Might be the other way around," Lyle said.

Blake stood too close for the standards of polite society, let alone a prison guard. More importantly: Francis allowed it. The man was addicted to his nicotine, but there were limits to how far even he would pretend to enjoy someone's company. Francis maintained eye contact throughout the conversation, only glancing over his shoulder every so often to look for guards like Hurst or Shepherd—either of which who would be far too happy to break up their little play date in the laundry room. Francis was invested like a shameless flirt.

Unless the kid was Francis' type in the other way.

While Lyle considered flirting accusations first, he really shouldn't overlook what really got Francis' blood pumping. Perhaps his nicotine-addicted friend allowed the guard's closeness to open up a chance to have some 'real fun,' as he had put it once. It wasn't like Blake had the self-preservation skills to step back if someone swung a shank at him. Lyle had heard plenty of stories about the Hackney Hacker, some before his arrest in the papers, and a few straight from the Hacker's mouth when he was feeling waxing poetic. The title and gory tales never seemed to fit the diminutive man with his constant dry wit, laid back nature, and familiar smell of smoke.

Lyle smoothed a crease in the fold of a shirt. Francis whispered in Blake's ear, with that crooked smile pulling at the side of his lips. Blake stiffened, before he said something back right back accompanied by a smack to the smoker's shoulder. Francis flinched, before looking off to the side to cover his mouth and laugh. The motion was casual, but Lyle could see it—the excitement. The twitch in Francis' fingers. The curve of his lips.

They giggled like schoolgirls, but Francis was a viper posed to strike.

Lyle folded faster, something unsettling in his stomach. Francis was either going to kill that kid, or shove his face into a mattress. At this point, it was impossible to tell which way a killer like Francis would lean. Who knew how their minds were wired? Until the smoker made a move, Lyle could only consider the various options. Whatever happened, the tension between those two was as plain as day for anyone who cared to look. You could feel it around them like a drawn out wire trap.

"You guys hear what happened in J-Block?"

Lyle slipped, the sleeve of the shirt dropping out of its neat fold. A guy from the second floor of G-Block put himself between Lyle and his view of Blake and Francis' odd dance. Lyle hadn't bothered to learn the man's name. He did take the time to find out what the guy was put away for, though. The man killed his wife's exes—all six of them.

The man continued on, with or without Lyle's answer to his question. "They're super pissed off about Brandy going to solitary for two months. They said that B-Block pansy had his killin' coming."

"What do we care about it?" Lyle fixed the fold on his shirt, and pulled another shirt from the basket. He avoided eye contact. Lyle already had his murderer and lunatic quotas filled when it came to friends. The other man sweated as he leaned over the table, clutching a bundle of dirty clothes. He trembled, fingers spastic around the fabric under his hands. Vernon watched them both, the shaking in his hands increasing. The Six-Man-Killer's nervousness was contagious. Lyle placed a shirt over the table, and grabbed Vernon's hand underneath. He interlaced their fingers, and squeezed. Vernon calmed minutely, but Lyle would take what he could get. "Best to stay out of their business, if you ask me."

28

"I mean they're really, really pissed." The guy continued, glancing between the two. He spoke in a hushed hiss that sparked a flare of unease in Lyle's mind. "They said they're going to get revenge. They're taking it all the way to the top."

"To the Warden?" Lyle asked. "Are you serious?"

"Yeah," He bit his lip, looking around for the other guards. Hyena Hurst was lurking around earlier, and punishing gossip was near the top of his favorite list of offenses. The man backed up from the table, forcing eye contact with Lyle. "I'd watch your back tonight. Spread the word."

"I'll keep that in mind," Lyle said, letting go of Vernon's hand. The man from the second floor went to the next table, starting his trembling speech over. True or not, rumors like that led to trouble.

Vernon folded his shirts, mumbling about Jack and Julie fighting against a vengeful Max. The thought of a break out must have been too much for him. Lyle placed a hand in his friend's greasy hair, and rubbed gently as Vernon sunk further and further into his own made up little world.

Francis laughed across the room, lighting up a fresh cigarette, oblivious to the warnings his work table had been granted. Blake shook his head, snatching it back an inch from the lit tip. He tapped Francis' shirt with the back of his knuckles in a harmless wrist slap for smoking in the laundry room. Francis retaliated. He grabbed Blake's wrists to pull the guard's hands near his face, and used his mouth to retrieve the cigarette with his teeth. Francis released the guard laughing, pausing just long enough to blow smoke in the kid's face. Blake waved away the smoke smiling before lightly punching the smoker in the upper arm.

Lyle saw it.

Blake blushed with Francis' mouth that close to his hand. Lyle plucked a piece of lint off the shirt he held. He had tensed, ready for something else.

If it wasn't one thing, it was another. Lyle cupped the back of Vernon's head as he mumbled. Lyle watched Francis and Blake stand too close. Be too close. The game between them was coming to a head, escalating into something bigger that would break one way or the other.

Tonight was the night—but for which, he didn't know. Lyle could feel it. Like the split-second before the cops appeared around the corner of his get-away car. He could *feel* it. Francis and Blake would go to the next level—be it sex or murder—or the prisoners in J-Block were going to

29

throw a mutiny. Lyle folded the next shirt, and stuck it in the pile next to Vernon's.

Whichever one decided to rear its ugly head tonight, Lyle would be ready for it.

CHAPTER 6

SOMETHING WAS WRONG.

Francis could feel it radiating in his gut, suffocating his lungs far more than any inhale of smoke. It was there in the room: A lurking quiet under the regular night noises of shuffling and creaking walls. Everyone retained their disguise of the ordinary, but they knew it was there. Like a swarm of gnats crawling under their skin. The guards walked a tad too stiffly, and the inmates hung a tad too close to the bars as they went about their normal routines. No one knew what was exactly about to go down, but they could sense it as easily as he could. Taste it. Francis clutched his last cigarette in his palm, smashed against his box of matches.

He'd already burnt through his entire new pack.

It was ten until lights out, and Ollie was making his last cell check before switching off with the night shift. He was one cell down saying goodnight before he'd reach Francis and Coal—he always saved them for last. Coal rarely talked, which left him plenty of time to finish up his shift with Francis while the second floor checks were completed. Francis could hear the guard above him tapping on the metal catwalk above, banging his baton against each and every cell bar. The clangs were steady as he dawdled along.

Ollie stopped in front of his cell. He was the epitome of calm—just another normal night to the kid. No one ever told the guards the rumors. Nothing that Chaplin had heard or shared in the Laundry Room made it to them. Francis should have taken Chaplin more seriously when he went back to folding clothes and received the second-hand message. Ollie couldn't feel it. He didn't have that instinct in his gut wriggling like worms to let him know shit was about to go down. In this rotting building full of corruption and bad men, Ollie was this absurd oddity of good and it played havoc with Francis' blood pressure.

Francis rolled off the bed, and leaned on the bars. "Evenin' kid."

"Francis, how are you?" Oliver asked, pleasant as always. He nodded his head toward a few cells down. "I noticed you and Chaplin were having a nice chat during laundry. He read a new book or something?"

"Nah," Francis said, licking his lips. The air was still with that calm in the center of a storm that fooled folks into leaving their houses too early before the worst of it struck. Ollie needed to leave. Now. "But he did say he was looking for something to read to Coal."

Coal was asleep already. The crazy had a better sense of self preservation than the smiling pup in front of him. It figured. Francis grabbed the bar and leaned on it, he kept his voice low to a whisper. He didn't want to set off the fireworks early on accident. "Your shift is almost up, right?"

"Yes, just like every night." Ollie scrunched his eyes together, suspicious of Francis' odd behavior. He never whispered like this until they had at least gotten talking for a few minutes. This wasn't going the way Francis wanted it. The guard above him clanked his baton louder. Or it just seemed louder. Maybe it was Francis' heart pounding harder for every second the kid stayed in the line of fire. Ollie brushed his bangs to the side of his head under the bill of his security cap. "I'm actually a little early, so there's no rush."

"I'm tired tonight, kid. Maybe you should go ahead and check out for the night." If he left now, Ollie had a good chance to be back in his safe little townhouse before everything hit the fan. Sure, all the inmates would head there first for revenge and giggles, but at least Ollie'd hear the commotion early instead of being stuck in the middle of it. He'd have time to prepare, or hide, or at the very least run. Time Ollie wouldn't have if he got caught in the middle of the prison riot with folks like Francis. "I'm sure your partner would appreciate the early check out."

"Are you alright?" Ollie asked. He stuck his hand threw the bar, and Francis backed up when it looked like Ollie was going to check his forehead for a temperature with the back of his hand. He made it to his bunk before the hand could make contact. Ollie drew his hand back and crossed his arms. He went into mother hen mode—another thing Francis didn't need right now. "You're sweating. Do you want me to escort you to the clinic?"

"No, I'm fine." Francis shook his head. He wiped his forehead with the sleeve of his jacket. It came back damp. *Perfect.* "Just tired, so go on home now."

"Are you sure? It's no trouble, and I'm done for the night, like I said."

"I'm sure, now get going so I can get some sleep." *Why won't he take a hint?* Francis picked up his empty pack of cigarettes and tossed it back and forth between his hands. His lone cigarette sat uselessly on his pack of matches. He turned his back to Ollie, and faced the wall. "Why don't you go do the same, 'kay?"

Ollie grabbed the bar with one hand with the worry written all over his face, laced with a hint of hurt. "What's wrong with you?"

No sooner had he finished his question, the lights went out. In a single sweeping click, it blanketed the entire area in black. Four flashlights blinked on, two on the bottom floor, and two above on the catwalks. Their warm yellow light crisscrossed over the room, searching for the source of the darkness. Francis popped his cigarette in his mouth, and shoved his matches in his pockets.

Shit decided to go down.

CHAPTER 7

OLIVER SWUNG THE flashlight beam over the inmates. They climbed out of their beds to hang at their bars, slowly and surely like the undead discovering the soil above their heads had been removed. Oliver tightened the grip on his flashlight. The tapping of shined shoes clicked as Johnson trotted up beside him. Collin and Simmons leant over the edges of their respective railings on the second floor catwalks, nothing but beams of light shooting out from darkness.

Johnson's harried brown eyes looked over each cell as his flashlight beamed down the line. He stepped closer to Oliver, his body language tense. Johnson bumped his elbow against Oliver's and said, "You think it's a black out, Blake?"

"No," Oliver said. He shined his flashlight up at the overhead pendant lamp. The light reflected off the white, coated surface of the round fixture. "The back-up generator would have come on. I think someone turned the lights off."

"Cut the power off, you mean," Francis said. He stood an inch from his bars, body tense, breath heavy and eyes focused. Francis' sweat from earlier might not have been from illness as he had first thought. Oliver's breath caught in the odd intensity radiating from Francis' relaxed posture. He had never wished so badly that Francis had just caught a cold. Oliver bit the edge of his lip as the older man pointed at the front guard station with his unlit cigarette. "Your cameras aren't blinking up there. If it were just the lights, those would be on, wouldn't they?"

Observant.

It was Oliver's favorite thing about Francis. The man had an eye for detail that showed up in his humor and his planning. It was a shame he used his skills to hunt people down and kill them instead of making things better. For now though, Oliver planned to make use of whatever he could, and that included Francis. He was someone Oliver could trust —someone with instincts.

He hoped.

Oliver swapped his flashlight to his left hand, so his right was free to rest on his pistol. Johnson shifted, the shuffling of his clothes echoing loudly in the quiet of the room. Oliver squeezed his pistol holder, the weight of it doubled on his side in the dark. "You're right. Something has to be wrong with the power."

A loud clang echoed in the empty room. A familiar sound Oliver knew well. They heard it twice a day at lunch and again during yard time: the sound of the cell door release. Oliver cursed under his breath, and braced his feet apart in a better stance. The cell doors were on their own panel and circuit. It wouldn't be hard to cut the power to everything else, while leaving those alone. Johnson took a step back, swinging his flashlight across the room wildly. Far too early, the cell doors slid open in unison. The metal creaked until everything settled into silence. Johnson shook in place, the objects on his belt clicking together with the vibrations.

"Shit," Francis said, gazing warily at the open space between him and Oliver. He put his cigarette in the corner of his mouth, and Oliver swore he saw the man's pupils dilate. Francis looked at Johnson and chuckled. "That ain't good for you guys."

"Everyone stay in your cells! That's an order!" Simmons shouted from just above their heads. He slammed his baton on the upper floor railing, shattering the momentary peace of their confusion. Oliver took a few steps back to shine his flashlight up and see him more properly. Simmons' mouth was twisted into a snarl, and his eyes were as violent as half the inmates Tobias Memorial had locked away. Simmons smacked the railing again, sending the metallic ringing around the room. He radiated authority, making sure everyone's eyes were on him. "I repeat, do not leave your cells, and stay exactly where you are!"

For now, they listened. Oliver saw bit lips, and constantly moving eyes on the inmates shifting in place behind the wide-open space where their doors used to be. The threat of violence in Simmons' voice and posture were more than enough to keep them all in place.

At least until the loudspeaker clicked on.

"My fellow inmates," a calm voice echoed through the tinny speakers. The gruff and unfamiliar gravely tone sent goosebumps over Oliver's arms under his thick jacket sleeves. "As of right now, our dear Brandy has been released from solitary, and I am pleased to inform you the unfair punishment dealt to him has been paid back in full. The Warden is dead, the lines to the mainland have been cut, and your cells have been opened. Have fun."

Hell broke loose in the room like a wildfire.

CHAPTER 8

FRANCIS GRABBED OLLIE'S collar and yanked him into the cell without a second thought. He shoved the young man behind him and onto his knees facing the wall. The tension snapped like a trip wire. The other inmates exploded from their cells like water rushing out of a broken dam, pouring out to flood the towns below. Francis pushed Ollie's head down, and blocked his peripheral with a knee. No reason the kid should have to see Francis' cellmates beat Ollie's partner with his own baton until there was nothing left of the man's head but a bloody paste.

Kid was sensitive.

The upper catwalk rattled, as feet smashed against the metal and the guards were overthrown. Ollie shook like a shivering wretch under him. Francis waited. And watched.

The second floor guard from the opposite side fell over the railing, smashing into the concrete floor with a crack. Grey matter from the impact speckled Johnson sprawled out a couple feet away. The usually tired face of Ollie's partner was puffed with bruises and knots, and while they didn't go as far as to turn his head into a paste as predicted, he was still very, very dead. Francis searched the corpse with his eyes, and his hand still holding the trembling Ollie in place. His breath picked up as the scent of iron and salt reached his nose.

The guards' guns were missing.

Francis grabbed Ollie's waistline, feeling his belt—Ollie's was not. As Francis breathed a sigh of relief, a guard hat dropped just outside his cell. From above came quiet pleading, and the shifting of metal under moving feet. Francis knew the tell-tale signs of a deal being cut when he heard it.

During a break out, a dirty guard could be an inmate's best friend.

They had keys, access to the weapons, and keeping in mind most of them were as rotten as the inmates—a good ally. What better place than Tobias Memorial to find one of those? Save for the shaking kid Francis had shoved against a wall, that is. Francis' little exception.

Ollie's kind nature was hated in a place like this far more than it was loved, by guards and inmates alike. Kid was too sensitive. Francis cursed and wondered yet again how he got here. Ollie didn't have the stomach for this place, and it was never more obvious than right now. Shepherd, regrettably, had likely been the only thing protecting the kid. Now that the hierarchy was thrown to the wolves, they'd eat Ollie alive if he was caught out there trying to create order like he did in the damn yard during the fight that caused all this.

Francis' grip on the kid's arm went from secure to death tight. There'd be a bruise there, but pain was a good reminder. Francis hissed in the kid's ear. "You listen good, Ollie. As of right now, you stick with me. You do what I say, when I say it—no hesitation. You got that?"

Ollie's face contorted in frustration, his eyes wet and *angry*. Francis heart beat a notch faster seeing the intensity of it. He couldn't ever remember seeing the kid angry. Maybe angry enough to do something— but Ollie wasn't that stupid. He knew what was going on. He'd listen to Francis. The kid rubbed his mouth with the back of his hand, and calmed his breathing. His shaking slowed to stillness. A determination settled over the kid that reminded Francis of himself before a kill. His body tightened like a coiled spring. It was a good look on Ollie.

The kid met Francis' eyes, that olive green dark pooling with heat. "I understand."

"We wait fifteen minutes." Francis knelt on one knee, clenching the cigarette between his teeth. He kept an eye on the entrance to his cell, but the rioting inmates were ignoring him for now. They probably remembered his Hacker stories and knew to stay clear. *Good*. The metal above their heads rattled with the heavy thuds of footsteps. "Those that are going to make a break for it'll be gone in less than ten. We can deal with the folks who're hanging behind after, and sort out our allies from the worthless. We're not exactly pushovers in here, but I sure as hell don't want to run into some of the folks from the other blocks alone right now."

"What do you think happened?" Ollie asked under his breath. He shifted so he could put an arm up on the bunk and see out into the block. Francis knew when he spotted Johnson by the way Ollie's fingers twitched, the way his breath hiccuped. None of the shock leaked into his voice. "I didn't recognize the voice on the loudspeaker. Did you?"

"Someone from J-Block, I'd assume, if they were avenging the guy from the yard the other day." Francis left Ollie's side, stretching his arms over his head as he stood. He stretched out his calves by leaning over and running his hands down his legs. More limber than before, he poked his head out of the cell.

It smelled like death.

Blood covered every surfa—Francis couldn't go there. He sucked in a breath, tilting his head back. Francis thought of smoke and concrete floors. Grey. Dull things. He couldn't see red. Francis couldn't keep Ollie alive if he acknowledged red.

Francis kept his eyes above floor level. He stared at the catwalks. The grey. "Don't ask me how they managed it, though."

"Force, most likely." Francis heard from two cells down. Chaplin walked out of his cell, his figure even more tall and imposing than usual in the emptied room. Coal shuffled out from his own hidey-hole and raced over to his friend. Chaplin kicked Johnson's leg before shoving his hands in his pocket, not even blinking when Coal attached himself to the taller man's waist. "Security was always lousy. I'm more surprised this didn't happen sooner."

Francis should have known those two would stick with him. "Boys."

"See you saved the kid," Chaplin said, nodding his head toward Ollie lingering in the back of the cell. Francis didn't appreciate the way Chaplin looked down at the kid, sizing him up. Debating if Ollie was a liability. It was all there in the bald man's eyes. Francis really didn't want to know what would happen if he had to pick between the kid and Chaplin. With his size and experience, the man was an ally Francis couldn't afford to lose right now. Chaplin crossed his arms across his chest. "Was that wise? Babysitting him could cost us."

Ollie straightened as tall as he could. A useless gesture, even as he walked out of the cell to defend himself. Chaplin still had a good sixty pounds and a foot on him. Ollie squared his shoulders. "I'm not a child."

"You are to us. Green in every way that matters." Francis said. "But you're coming either way, so let's get moving before someone comes hunting us down."

Francis walked out of his cell, taking the lead as usual. He avoided the bodies of the two guards, going a full two feet around them and out of his way. *Don't look at the blood. Don't look at the blood. Don't look at the blood.* Chaplin grabbed the hand of his own childish charge and followed along as they past the scattered mess the inmates left of the front desk. Coal didn't complain, but he did manage to mumble something about Jack and Julie hooking up. Francis had wondered when that was going to happen.

Better late than never.

Francis smirked, eyeing the twitching burden behind Chaplin. There was no way that big lug could complain about Ollie when he was dragging around Coal. Francis was not beneath pointing it out either if it came to that. He'd kill Coal long before he let anything happy to Ollie. Chaplin jerked his hand, pulling said charge to the main doors.

They stopped at the main door, one last time before braving the outer hall and whatever awaited them.

Chaplin said, "I think heading for the boats is our best bet. If we get there soon enough, we might be able to take one over, or catch a ride on the one already heading out."

Francis was proud Ollie knew to keep his mouth shut about the escape plan, even if he couldn't hide the disapproving frown. Hopefully Ollie could remain a tagalong, and not have to worry about getting his hands dirty. Poor kid would probably have a panic attack, and Francis had no desire to knock him out and drag him around if Ollie could walk on his own.

It wouldn't come to that.

Francis smacked the largest of their group in the arm, and pointed his thumb over his shoulder. "Don't forget to grab that guy's baton, Chaplin."

The group of four exited G-Block, heading into the main 'street' of the prison. The long corridor was sparse and empty, save for the double-doors that lead to each Block lining the walls. There were five to each side, ten blocks in all. Painted green, chipped and dull as the rest of the atmosphere in this place. With the power out, and the dark looming, it was like walking through a horror flick with salvation at the end. To one side, the entrance to the prison's yard. To the other, was an adjoining building that housed the cafeteria, library, laundry, activity areas, and B-Block's precious rose courtyard in the center of the square. Past that were the guard quarters and more importantly, the docks.

Salvation.

Francis chewed the end of his cigarette, tasting flakes of tobacco and tar on his tongue. Their steps echoed as they walked steadily down the row. Darkness led their way, and even the cameras that dotted the upper walls stood dormant. Not a blinking red light to be seen.

For a prison break, it was oddly quiet.

"Everyone must have made a dash for the front," Ollie said absently, eyes scanning the empty hall. He stayed close to Francis' side opposite Chaplin and Coal, steps hesitant and unsure. He looked like kid tip-toeing around his house so his folks wouldn't catch him sneaking out of bed. Ollie squinted into the darkness of A-Block, his flashlight off to keep from attracting too much attention from the crazies lurking beyond the doors. "Or are hiding in their cells."

"Both is likely," Francis said. He walked down the corridor at a steady pace, strides long and confident. Unlike the kid, he had nothing to be afraid of. Francis was the predator. The Hacker. It was the other inmates who should be running from *him*.

Francis dragged Ollie forward by the sleeve to keep him up with the pace. He didn't want the kid lagging behind with Chaplin and Coal. "Let's move. Hopefully they're not crowding the docks like animals."

It was the sound that stopped them all in their tracks.

Francis heard it first, recognizing the pleasant reverberations of muffled agony. The reinforced double doors at the end of the reaching hallway hung open. An invitation. Francis was the first to move, as the others tagging along reluctantly. The closer they approached, the more obvious the pained sobbing became. Some poor sap ran into the wrong person at the wrong time.

Francis grabbed Ollie's arm instinctively. Again. The boy growled at him, already mid-step in a rush to help. He tried to tug his arm out of the grip, but Francis held tight. He couldn't give two shits about the kid's ethics code. There was not a chance in hell they were getting involved with what was going on past that doorway.

Francis pulled Ollie close, changing his grip to the upper arm. "We wait for the nice killer to finish, and then we walk by him while he licks up. Do you understand me?"

Ollie trembled under his hold as the echoing sobs morphed into pained screaming. The kid's eyes widened, and every muscle in the slim body tensed in preparation. There was no doubt: the second Francis let go, Ollie'd go running. Francis squeezed harder, as Chaplin judged—staring down disapprovingly. Francis wasn't letting go of Ollie.

After an eternity of waiting, listening to the carnage and his own blood screaming for Francis to join in, there was a final wet plop. Heavy air settled in their lungs, pressing and tense. Silence followed for an agonizing minute, as the group waited for what came next.

Footsteps tapped along the concrete floors, bringing their mystery killer into view. The man's pristine black uniform was coated in blood. A dulled copper color soaked into the thick fabric. Human rust. A switchblade hung lightly in the limp hand extending from the wet sleeve. The madman's smile was deceptively pleasant—a familiar look on Guard Emmanuel Shepherd.

Ollie covered his mouth to hide the unintentional gasp. Francis narrowed his eyes.

Like he had said before: *A killer knew a killer.*

"Inmate Francis Ellis Hackney," Shepherd said, standing at attention as if the red staining his suit didn't exist. His blond hair was striped in strawberry, slicked down by a blood-soaked hand. Shepherd held his arm out to Ollie, as if he were indicating an art piece on display. "Now where might you be taking my subservient little Oliver?"

Francis shoved Ollie behind him where Lyle had stashed Coal. The two of them huddled behind Francis and Chaplin standing shoulder to shoulder. Forming a unified front with Lyle was easy when you had the same goal. Francis brandished his baton, keeping his eye on the gun sitting on Shepherd's belt. *Should have taken Ollie's. Stupid. Stupid. Stupid.* "Just keep walking, Shepherd."

"Nonsense. You're holding my friend captive." Shepherd said, as pleasantly as if he were turning down a spot of tea. He smiled, his teeth an unnatural shade of white sticking out from a face covered in dark red. Everything about Shepherd was warped. Even his posture spoke of the unwell without a single word. "Why would I allow such a thing?"

"He's not your friend, and we both know it," Francis said.

"I think our little visits over tea and supper would say otherwise, Inmate Francis Ellis Hackney." Shepherd's grip on his knife tightened, his voice strained.

Shepherd cracked, chipped as his china cups.

Francis held his hand out to block Ollie when he took a stupid step forward ahead of Coal. "Kid, stay put."

"But," Ollie said. He pulled on Francis' sleeve. Ollie's face went back and forth between a forced smile and pained fear as his mind struggled to process what he was seeing. Ollie shook his head, his grip on the fabric sleeve pulsing. "That's Em. It—there has to be some mistake. We should talk this out."

"No can do, kid." Francis elbowed Ollie back into Coal. Chaplin made eye contact with Francis, and pushed his friend into Ollie. He took the hint. "We're not doing anything but leaving."

Shepherd's pleasant smile contorted through the shock and rage until it fell into a twisted scowl. He raised the knife fast enough that it cut the air with an audible swipe. He pointed it straight to the center of Francis' heart. "The boy wants nothing to do with you, Inmate Francis Ellis Hackney. Now give me Guard Oliver Blake."

"Not happening, buddy-boy," Francis said. Now that Shepherd was finished with whatever sap that painted the guard red, he was looking for a new toy, and Francis already had dibs on this one. He grabbed Ollie's arm and ran forward at top speed. Chaplin and Coal would figure it out. They'd been around each other long enough to get that far at least. Francis laughed when Chaplin pushed ahead and body slammed the lithe guard into the sidewall, smearing blood on them both.

Shepherd stumbled on his feet, but stayed upright leaning on the brickwork. He made a swipe for Chaplin with his blade, but the big man had never stopped moving. The group ran past the blood soaked guard without so much as a hitch.

"Get back here!" Shepherd shrieked, waving his knife in the air. His pupils constricted to the size of pin-points as the veins pulsed in his neck. "Give me back Guard Oliver Blake! He's mine!"

Francis slammed the hallway door shut on the man before he could catch up. He threw the manual bolt lock into place, securing it. Shepherd banged on the glass, unhinged as a shoddy birdcage door. Power'd been out less than an hour and he was already a magnificent, spitting, psychopathic mess.

It was beautiful.

Ollie squeezed Francis' hand. His trembling form distracted, and Francis turned away. Ever inch of his willpower wanted to turn right back around and tackle Shepherd to the ground. But Ollie, and...*So much red.* Francis laced his fingers through Ollie's and held tight.

"Always knew that guy was nuts," Chaplin said, keeping his eyes behind them. He rubbed Coal's back, as they moved away from the rattling door where Shepherd continued to beat the glass.

"Let's go before the rest of the guards start showing their true colors," Francis said airily. Shepherd screamed muffled obscenities, the heavy door turning them into unintelligible gibberish.

Ollie knocked into his side, trembling. Francis forgot the metallic pounding and muffled screams in the background as he steadied the little guard. Ollie was paler than Shepherd, hyperventilating into the hands covering his mouth. Francis smiled fondly, rubbing the kid's back. "Yeah, yeah. Your buddy's crazy. We should probably get going, kid."

"Why aren't you surprised?" Ollie asked, as Francis pulled him down the hallway and further away from the main hall doorway. Shepherd's pounding faded into the background as scattered voices filled the area. Francis kept his grip on Ollie's hand. Shepherd was the big gun, but a whole lot of little guns could be just as bad just as quick in a mob. Ollie squeezed his hand as they approached the corner of the hallway. "I've never seen Em that way before."

"You learn to sense your own real quick," Francis grinned. Shepherd's enraged face flooded his vision. Twisted, snarling, and the promise of murder in every contorted wrinkle in his pale skin. Francis' heart skipped a beat. *Blood, blood, blood.* "And in here, that's pretty much everyone."

Chaplin rolled his eyes as he pushed Coal along. The shaking inmate stumbled, his eyes dashing everywhere. It was a little hilarious. Francis laughed, and wrapped his arm around Ollie's shoulders. He was as bad as Coal, shivering and looking over his shoulder in a new sort of shock. Truth. Francis pulled Ollie in tight under his wing, and thumped the kid's chest. Francis' hand hit hard against something just under the jacket—a thick vest. *Bullet proof?* How long had the guards been hiding those?

Francis lightly cuffed Ollie's cheek, happy the kid had some protection. His hand-to-hand was worthless. "You're the only good guy around here, remember?"

"That's not true," Ollie said. He huffed, shoving at Francis' arm. It was as effective at escaping Francis' headlock as a toddler was escaping an older sibling pulling the same stunt. Francis was on top of the world when Ollie gave up and settled against Francis' chest, exasperated. "The guards here are my friends."

"No, they played nice with you because they knew better. Hate to break it to you, but if Shepherd didn't scare the hell out of all your 'friends,' they would have eaten you alive the first chance they got," Francis said, his voice a touch too chipper even for his own sake. He needed to get it together. Francis placed his back flat against a wall with Ollie still tucked neatly into his chest. Francis almost hated how much he loved the way the kid shivered.

Almost.

Francis peered around the corner, distracting himself. A few inmates fought with each other surrounding by a crowd of gawkers, their hooting and hollering carrying the entire way down the corridor. Two others were huddled in a corner, cheering. Nothing he and Chaplin couldn't handle. He slapped Ollie on the back and pushed the kid off his chest. Francis flexed his fingers. "Most of the guards are as bloodthirsty as the rest of us when you get down to it."

"But you're not bad," Ollie said, crossing his arms against his chest. He rubbed the sleeve like it was snowing and he'd forgotten his mittens. "We've gotten to know each other pretty well, I mean—"

"Ollie, kid," Francis said, odd smile crooked on his mouth. He lightly smacked the kid's cheek with the base of his palm. A humoring gesture if there ever were one. "I'm a serial killer. Pretty sure that that disqualifies me from being 'not bad,' don't you think?"

The kid kept silent, his head toward the ground in deep though. His whole world was crumbling, wasn't it? Francis knocked Ollie's hat off with a flick of his fingers, and ruffled the kid's hair hard enough to dig his fingers into the kid's scalp. Morose wasn't a good look on Ollie. "Makes me wonder what goes on in that head of yours to have thought otherwise for so long."

Ollie opened his mouth, and shut it soundly. He reached down for his cap and shoved it back on his head. Francis hadn't expected an answer, anyway.

He rubbed the base of his palm against his nose in a huff. If they lived through this, he doubted Ollie would keep buying him smokes. "Let's go."

CHAPTER 9

LYLE TOOK THE lead.

It was the most logical decision. He was the tallest and fiercest-looking, even though their impromptu leader was the most dangerous. It was easy to forget the smoking addict was a vicious serial killer when he spent his time fawning over a stumbling brat like a lovesick teenager. Vernon knocked into his side as he walked an inch too close. The corners of the man's eyes twitched, and he chewed the side of his thumb around his mumblings. Lyle sighed, straightening out his jacket. He couldn't talk much, could he?

Francis instructed Blake to walk shoulder to shoulder with the rest of them as calmly as he could fake it as they passed through the dining hall. Guards siding with the inmates around here would get a glance, but no one would think twice on it. The worthless ones, or the ones inmates had grudges with were long gone. However, Francis still kept Blake to the center next to Vernon, far away from the inmates that removed themselves from Lyle's path. Francis' glare was a larger deterrent than Blake's failed attempts at looking calm any way.

Lyle was surprised so many of their peers were still hanging out in the main building. They were scattered among the turned over tables in groups of three or four, the usual cliques that he'd often see in the yard hanging together. They ignored the splatters of blood against the spotless white tables and aged blackened brick alike, as well as the occasional unmoving body like it was a spilled over food tray. Friendly brawls and men hanging out—nothing like the mad dash for the docks he'd been expecting.

Lyle held tight to his confiscated baton. He'd never liked the unexpected.

"Folks like Shepherd don't sit still for long unless everyone is dead," Francis said. He nodded toward a side door that led to the facility gates. Lyle kept a close watch on the man's body language. Francis' fingers twitched every so often. It usually coincided with the man overlooking a puddle of blood. Lyle nodded and changed his path to head for the doors.

Getting out into the fresh air had nothing to do with Shepherd catching up.

Lyle said, "We can get to the guard quarters through that gate exit using Blake's key. The docks aren't much further."

"Right," Francis agreed. He pushed ahead of Lyle and through the door like fire was nipping at his heels. Blake followed, close in tow.

A ten minute walk down the bumpy stone path later, and Blake's key to the gate turned out to be unnecessary. The security fence gate was destroyed. Ripped out of the ground, mangled and useless without its armed guards to defend it. Lyle hoped whoever was responsible for this had passed by the townhouses and headed straight for the docks, but even he didn't think they'd be that lucky.

"You hanging in there, Ollie?" Francis asked, his eyes softer now that the remnants of human violence were behind closed doors. "I doubt the guard quarters are going to look better than the rest of this place."

Blake took his cap off and scratched the back of his head. He asked, "Do you think the inmates would leave the families alone?"

Even as he asked it, Lyle knew Blake was grasping at straws. Only a third of the guards actually had wives and kids on the island, but it was enough. Folks like Shepherd and Francis couldn't help themselves, and Lyle knew there was more than one child killer in Tobias Memorial. Blake at least knew that much, too.

"I'm sure the guards with kids went home the second the lights went out," Francis said, the offer slim. It was far more likely it was the first place the inmates with grudges went.

The sound of a slide loading a round was an unexpected reply.

CHAPTER 10

THE TOWNHOUSE DOORS hung open, some hanging off their hinges by a single screw.

Oliver shoved his pistol back into its holster, loaded and ready, but useless. He'd done well all the times he'd practiced shooting with Johnson at the range, but Oliver had been calm, cool and collected during those sessions. But that had been target practice against pieces of paper. Not people. And besides, the silence and blood spatters that covered the sidewalks and townhouse stoops were more than enough to communicate there was no one left to save. Francis lifted an eyebrow, no doubt thinking it unwise to put up the weapon.

He was probably right.

Oliver passed Em's quarters and wrinkled his nose at the broken china pieces covering the front steps. Mutilated and smashed cups were strewn everywhere on the floor, spilling out into the open on the step. Through the open door, Oliver could see the painting of the woman in flowers on the floor, the canvas ripped open in tattered strips. Pieces of broken plates were smashed beneath it, the slivers of multi-colored bone china covering the ground like the flower petals in the painting. If Francis had been wrong about Em being a psychopath during his entire campaign as guard, Oliver believed this would have been enough to drive him to that point.

Em was crazy about his china.

Oliver stepped over a chipped cup as he continued the walk down the strip, looking in each doorway for a hidden inmate. The townhouse row looked deserted, but after the past few hours, one could never be too careful. Chaplin and Francis were a bit more proactive, physically going up the stoop of each door and taking a peak around the rooms to double check. Coal huddled at the step of each one, waiting for Chaplin to come back out.

Feeling safe that his back was taken care of, Oliver proceeded to his own home. His door was broken in half at the center, kicked in if he had to guess. He tipped the lower half of his door fully off his stoop with the edge of his shoe. The hinge fell off, clanging to the concrete a few feet below the stairs. Oliver entered, leaving the safety of his group for a moment.

"Where you going, Ollie? We don't have time to check victims, and there's nothing hiding in there you should see first if you know what I mean," Francis said. His concern wormed its way into Oliver's chest, a warm feeling. Francis tossed the remains of his chewed cigarette to the ground with a huff. "Ollie?"

"Just a second, there's something I need to get first," Oliver said, from the doorway. He glanced around the overturned table and chairs of the main room. The damage wasn't as bad as he was expecting. A chair leg was broken off, and the kitchen lamp was on the coffee table, but there wasn't much else to damage. He was never that big on decorating. "It'll only take a second."

Oliver set the table back upright, and set the Bible that had been thrown off back in its proper place. The feel of the worn leather lingered on his fingertips as Oliver stood. Francis stepped into the room, and Oliver put the book in the opening of his jacket. He let the thin tome settle snug in place just above his belt.

"You really think we have time for that, Ollie?" Francis looked around the room, eyes lingering on an overturned cup on the kitchen counter. A package of opened crackers and jam were splattered over the countertop, and the half-eaten crumbs and sticky mess stained his countertop. Oliver hoped Francis realized that was due to the unexpected guests, and not his housekeeping.

He was raised better than that.

"It belonged to my big brother, and I'm not sure if it'll be here next time I am," Oliver said over his shoulder. Francis snorted and helped himself to a cracker from the torn package. He leaned on the side counter, with his hip cocked at an angle, sticking the square in his mouth using his thumb and forefinger. He brushed the crumbs out of the side of his mouth with the tip of his thumb. Oliver stared at the familiar motion.

The familiar pose.

Just like dad.

"I just need one more thing and we're done," Oliver said, covering his mouth and pushing back toward the other half of the townhouse.

The back room door was open, and he could see his clothing spilling out of open drawers. A chest was knocked over on its sides, the contents covering the floor in a blanket of knick-knacks. Oliver didn't have much in the way of stealing, and he was sure the inmates discovered that fairly quickly.

Or nothing they'd find anyway.

Francis hung in the doorway of the bedroom as Oliver got down on his knees and stuck his hand under the bed. He felt around for the small box he had shoved up between the framing and the mattress, wincing when his finger caught on a loose nail. Oliver found it on a second grab, and it was freed with a quick tug. Oliver sat on top of his comforter with the treasure cradled in his lap.

The small cherry wood box was about as wide as two card decks placed end to end, and only about an inch thicker. Oliver flipped open the top, conscious of Francis watching over his shoulder. Inside was a rosary from his Catholic mother, and a regular simple wooden cross from his Protestant father. How the two had gotten together, Oliver had still never figured out. The last items lingering at the bottom of the case were a handful of small smooth stones he'd hunted out of a bin with his mother on a rare trip to a mall. Oliver closed the lid, and shoved the entire box into his inside coat pocket.

Francis watched him stand up and lifted an eyebrow. "That it?"

"Yes," Oliver said. He moved to join Francis when the bathroom door came into view. Oliver smacked his forehead, running his hand down his face. How could he forget Em's present? He tapped Francis' shoulder, sending him a sly smile. "No, sorry. One more thing."

"And what would that be?" Francis said, opening a drawer next to his bed. It was empty, Oliver knew. He had as much need for side tables as he did interior decorations. He disappeared into the bathroom while Francis continued his curious trek exploring Oliver's empty drawers. Francis knocked a shelf close with his knee. "Another little keepsake, maybe?"

"Nah, just this." Oliver came out of the bathroom carrying a double-barrel shotgun and a box of ammo.

Francis wolf-whistled.

Oliver smirked, the expression unfamiliar and odd on his own face. But he couldn't help it just this once. If Francis knew the shotgun was a gift from Em, he doubted that he'd be looking at it the way a starved man sees food. Em had helped him hide it in a cabinet that sat overtop the toilet a month ago. The top half held toiletries, but beneath was nothing but open space—the perfect place to hide a weapon. Oliver was glad Em insisted on him keeping it now that Francis continued to appreciate the weapon, his fingers itching. Oliver tossed the gun over, and Francis caught it with one hand.

Oliver never did have much use for it himself.

"You are full of surprises, aren't you?" Francis grinned, mouth quirking in that odd half-smile Oliver was so used to. So fond of. His stomach tied itself into knots at the sight, threatening to spread to his lungs and choke him. Oliver left the room with his hand covering his mouth, knowing Francis was at his back.

CHAPTER 11

EMMANUEL FOUND TEN other guards alive in the compound.

He rescued two from a pair of inmates who chose to indulge in their love of torture over delivering a quick death. The two guards were shaken, but getting themselves back together after being allowed access to the torn medical facilities. Six others were holed up in the garden with the inmates from B-Block. They held off their more vicious peers as best they were able, and were welcome to Emmanuel's assistance. They were soon wary of his blood-coated form, but wisely decided it was best to side with him over the prisoners.

He returned the inmates of B-Block promptly back to their cells and locked them in with a swift click of the closed manual doors. His rescued guards remained in the B-Block, guarding the double doors against intruders, and preventing a second escape. Emmanuel felt better having restored at least this much peace to the area.

The last two guards had sided with the inmates in their escape, one of them from his own G-Block. It was embarrassing. Disgraceful. Emmanuel killed them as excruciatingly as he was able. Bits and pieces of them decorated the walls and baskets of the laundry room. *Traitors.* They did however mention that Guard Liam Hurst was wandering about still, but Emmanuel chose not to count him.

He was unhinged.

Emmanuel returned to his stock of guards shortly after, and gave a single ultimatum: Lock up who you could, shoot who you couldn't.

With that, Emmanuel had one loose end to finish up: Find his dear, dear Guard Oliver Blake.

The boy was too naive, too *kind* to have betrayed their cause. Dear

Guard Oliver Blake was bewitched by the serial killer; it was the only explanation for constantly sneaking off with him. Inmate Francis Ellis Hackney was a poison, steadily driving dear Oliver to ruin. Emmanuel would kill the inmate, and retrieve his final living guard.

Emmanuel secured a rose to his lapel, the color a brilliant red. B-Block certainly knew how to care for their things, something Emmanuel admired. It was a much needed touch of elegance to balance out his brutality with no art to be fond in this gray and barren place. Emmanuel rubbed a petal between his fingers. Together with Oliver, they would slaughter any and every prisoner who didn't surrender.

Nothing would make him happier.

CHAPTER 12

LYLE DIDN'T LIKE waiting. He didn't trust Blake and Francis alone in the townhouse, and he certainly didn't trust being out in the open waiting for them. It had been quiet so far, but Lyle knew all about storms and how fast that could turn around. Your peaceful gray day turned to a torrent of wind and rain in the blink of an eye. Blake was the eye, and Francis was storm. It was a matter of time, really, like it always turned out to be. Just time.

Vernon crouched next to him, his fingers playing in the dirt. The jagged lines looked like lightning bolts in the brown soil, and Lyle had to wonder if his friend could tell what was coming, too. Vernon kept looking up and over his shoulder, his wild hair flying in every direction as he drew. He was. Vernon was waiting for something, and even in his madness still on the same page as Lyle.

"You okay, Vern?" Lyle asked, keeping his eye on the road. Keep the storm to your back, but be weary of newcomers and raiders.

"Yes," he answered, his voice hoarse and raw. His tiny form shook, shivering like a mouse. Vernon gripped his hair, smearing dirt into the black strands. He shook his head. "No. No, I...someone's watching us."

"Where?" Lyle asked. He and Vernon were really in sync today. "Did you see them?"

"Don't know, but I k-know." Vernon swayed as he stood, rubbing his arms. He scuffed out the dirt drawings with the tip of his ragged shoe, as he stared at something far in the distance. Eyes focused on something Lyle couldn't see. Did someone follow them? Vernon hissed, and every sound around them sounded ominous. Who knew what was hiding out there in the dark. "It's going to be bad."

"Don't worry, you've got me," Lyle said, meaning every word. He took Vernon's hand, and rubbed circles around his knuckles. "Okay?"

"I don't trust those two in there," Vernon said, twisting his head toward the townhouse. He bit his thumb on the free hand, gnawing on the edge. "It's like leaving Julie and Jack alone. They'll be up to something."

The sudden change in conversation wasn't unexpected, but the subject was. Lyle squeezed Vernon's hand, the clammy sweat slick against his own. "What makes you say that?"

"Francis'll pick the guard over us."

"I know," Lyle said, wrapping his fingers even tighter around Vernon's hand. He shifted and laced their fingers together, and tugged Vernon up off the ground to stand. Lyle brushed the dirt out of Vernon's hair, and left his hand in the dark, greasy strands. "That's why I'm here to look after you."

Vernon looked up, meeting him dead in the eyes. The awareness he saw in those dilated pupils shook Lyle to his core. Vernon closed the distance between their faces and whispered, "Then who'll look after *you?*"

Glass crunched behind them. The moment shattered and the two split apart. Lyle released Vernon's hand, and turned over to the townhouse. His palm felt cold. Lyle gripped his hands into fists to counteract it.

Blake tapped down the stairs with a strained look on his face that gave Lyle second thoughts about keeping this group of four together. Like he was weighed down by something. Every inch of his body language spoke of unease. The first sprinklings of rain to their little storm were already raining down on all their heads.

Francis followed, carrying something that there was no way Lyle was letting him keep.

CHAPTER 13

FRANCIS COULD TELL Chaplin was impressed with the shotgun. He took it away two seconds after seeing it, so it was either that, or he didn't trust Francis with it. The ease with which Chaplin checked the weapon for ammunition and tested the sights helped support the former hunch. Not being one for firearms in the first place, Francis didn't take it personally. He preferred knives himself, but he had a feeling Ollie wasn't going to hand over his Swiss Army Knife as easily as Francis had given up the shotgun.

Every good little boy scout needed a pocket knife.

"Keep your feet moving," Chaplin said, pushing ahead. The shotgun hung under his arm so naturally it was practically an extension of the man's self. He looked like an action hero from an old 90's movie—only sporting the latest prison fashion instead of a wife-beater. Chaplin patted the barrel of the weapon, pointed safely down at the paved road. "If we keep on this path we'll be to the docks in another twenty minutes."

"We're moving, we're moving," Coal said, and then repeated, "We're moving, we're moving."

Francis tapped his stolen baton against his shoulder. If they were really smart, they'd dump Coal off somewhere he couldn't hurt himself. If they did that though, Chaplin would likely make the same argument for Ollie, and then they'd have to hit each other. Depressingly, Coal was far more likely hold his weight if it came to a fight than Ollie, as crazy as he was. The guy was locked up in maximum security for more reasons than delusions.

Coal rubbed his hands together, as he shifted from one side of Chaplin to the other. "Moving, we're moving."

"Yes, yes. We're all moving." Francis wanted a cigarette. He regretted tossing the leftover stub earlier. He sorely missed its presence—lit or not. He rubbed his lips, and looked his shoulder. "Ollie, you still with us?"

"I never left," Ollie said, eyes down. His hand was over his chest, and Francis could see the boy rubbing the wooden box he'd rescued through the jacket fabric. He had an odd look on his face. Like he was thinking about something too hard. Francis didn't like it. Picking up on Francis' glare, Ollie sighed, "You'll have to forgive me if it's been a bad day."

"You kidding?" Francis asked, shoving his hands in his pockets. The stars glittered over his head, and the cool breeze felt good on his face. It had a nostalgic air to it, sneaking about in the dark. All Ollie needed was to lift his head up and appreciate what a beautiful night they had here. "This is turning out to be the best day of my life. Skipping out on a life sentence, watching sadistic guards get theirs, and the hope of living to slice another day? Ollie, kid, this is living!"

"They're just going to catch you again, and then what?"

Ollie stood straighter, and skipped ahead of the group, forcing them to a halt in the middle of the road. The kid sucked in a breath, and grabbed Francis' arm, facing him head on. It was a familiar stance he'd seen days before in the yard. That same disapproving face, daring to hold eye contact. Ollie was pulling Guard Mode during a break out. *Unbelievable.*

Francis crooked a condescending smile. "What are you doing, Ollie?"

"I think you should consider turning yourself in on the mainland, and claiming you only escaped to save your life." Ollie was as serious as the dead with every syllable.

"Your concern is adorable." Francis tapped the boy's cheek with the back of his knuckle, and put a hand over Ollie's still clenching his arm. The kid was cute when he was trying to give orders. "But that's not going to happen."

Ollie glared like an angry cat. "Do you really want to break out just to get caught again and make things worse?"

"I'm in jail for life, kid." Francis asked, as Ollie let him go and backed away. The kid had the nerve to clench his fists. "It really doesn't get much worse than that."

Ollie took his cap off, and rubbed a hand through his hair. Kid shook his head, clearing his thoughts, and replaced his hat on his head. He rubbed his face, as he started on ahead toward the docks again. "Just, please think about what you're doing. Things can always get worse, and I don't want to see anything happen to you."

"Why do you care so much about it?" Chaplin asked. The question almost stopped Francis in his tracks. It was something he'd wondered often at night, tossing his cigarettes back and forth—but never *asked*. He was never sure he wanted to know. Chaplin continued, "I know you're buddies with the guy, but you're almost over invested with him at this point."

"Yeah," Francis said, his voice oddly choked. The subject'd been broached and now it was in there. Wriggling through his brain and bursting free. Begging for attention. Francis whacked the baton hard against his shoulder, the resulting whack making Ollie flinch. The pain was distracting, but not enough. "Good point. Why *do* you care? It's not like you've been getting anything out of me for all those cigarettes you've snuck in."

Ollie paused for just a moment too long before he answered, "No reason."

Francis stopped walking, rigid on unfamiliar ground. *Ollie just lied to me.* Francis' stomach tightened, twisting into an odd sort of knot. The kind that weaseled its way up into your heart and head to strangle your vitals. The kid had never tried to pull one over on him before. He showed up with cigarettes, and asked for nothing in return but conversation. Company. Ollie was a good kid. He kept things to himself, sure, but he sure as hell didn't do things like *that*.

"Oliver," Francis said. The kid didn't stop walking. His pace increased instead, solidifying his guilt. Francis saw a different sort of red. "Oliver!"

Francis grabbed the kid's arm and swung him around. He got in Ollie's face, as close as they'd get hiding from the others in a corner. They were out in the open, but right now it felt like they were squeezed together in a coffin. Nose to nose, Francis' pulse increased erratically. He felt Ollie's blood pumping through the boy's skin. No Chaplin, no Shepherd, no Coal, no Hurst, nobody else—just a smoker and his source.

Francis hissed, "You do not *lie* to me."

Ollie sucked in a breath, swallowing air he shared with Francis. Kid shook like a trembling leaf, but he didn't answer.

Francis grabbed the lapel of Ollie's jacket, yanking the boy forward to the point that their noses brushed. "Oliver."

"I wanted to meet you," Ollie blurted. He pushed Francis' grip off his coat and took three or four steps back. The gap stretched like a cavern between them. Ollie clenched his fists, in and out. Nerves. Fear. Kid was terrified. Francis breathed harder as Ollie said, "That's all."

"Meet me?" Francis shook his head. He licked his lips, and rolled his fingers in a wave. They itched to grab Ollie again, and shake him back to normal. Where had all this come from? How did one stupid little question explode into this? Francis' voice hitched. "No, there's more to it than that. Why on earth would you want to meet me?"

Ollie studied a pebble under his shoe. His words were lighter than a breath hidden under the wind. "You're my big brother."

Francis couldn't have heard that correctly.

"Now you're messing with me, Ollie. Try again," he said. All Francis wanted was a different answer.

Any other answer.

"I'm not," Ollie said. Francis didn't get his answer. He tightened his grip on the baton, raising it an inch from his waist. Ollie held his hands up in front of his chest. His heel dug into the dirt, but his feet remained planted. Ollie hunched his shoulders, his eyes widening. "It's the truth!"

"Ollie," Francis said.

"You're my half-brother," Ollie said, shaking his head but keeping his gaze locked on Francis. He hugged his arms close to his chest, his voice shaking. Ollie's voice cracked, "We have the same father, I swear to you."

Ollie wasn't lying this time.

"No, that's impossible," Francis replied. Ollie wasn't lying, but who would tell the kid such *lies?* He crossed the ravine between them. Francis slammed the butt of his palm into Ollie's shoulder, shoving the kid back a few stumbling feet. Time to set the record straight. Francis couldn't believe Ollie would fall for shit like that. "Looks like someone pulled one over on you, kid. I killed my old man and his new fling in the same night. I think I'd know if he had another kid running around."

"I was at a friend's house. A sleepover." Ollie said, rubbing the spot Francis had struck him with the tips of his fingers.

"There was no other bedroom!" Francis smacked the baton against his own leg. The sting raced down the limb, grounding him. "Just a master with that bastard and some broad sleeping in it."

"I slept in the living room on the pull-out," the kid said, crossing his arms. Hugging himself. Ollie looked at the ground, a bit of anger showing on his face through the nerves. "We couldn't afford a bigger place!"

Ollie folded in on himself, as if he'd caught himself getting ready to fight back, and glanced around like a cornered rat, despite the open space all around him. He took a step back, to try and widen the little box he'd imagined around himself, and tripped on a loose rock. Francis's muscles tightened as Ollie crumpled to the ground in a pathetic heap. He cut his hand, and a red line split on his palm. *Red.* Francis sucked in a breath. Ollie breathed heavily at Francis' shoes as the inmate towered over him, both of them regaining their ground. Ollie opened his mouth to continue. Francis almost shoved Ollie's face into the dirt. He didn't want to hear the next part.

"Dad talked about you all the time. To friends, Mom, me. Always proud of his oldest." Ollie got to his knees, and he spoke to the dirt. There was something broken about the kid Francis hadn't seen before. His eyes focused on nothing, and everything. Understanding socked Francis at the belt line. Ollie pushed on the cut in his palm with his thumb. "I'm not surprised you didn't know he had another kid."

Francis could hear his breath, loud and heavy in the night air. Ollie pushed to his feet. He was lying. Francis shook his head. Had to be lying —but, the kid's face was just so open and pleading. He was good, really good. Francis hadn't given Ollie the credit he deserved. Maybe he did belong here on this wretched island with its corrupt guards and psychotic inmates after all.

He punched the kid hard enough to knock him flat on his back. Francis bit the back of his knuckle. "You're lying. You're lying and it ain't funny, Ollie!"

"I'm not." Ollie rubbed the blood from his split lip. He sat up, and reached into his jacket. Out came the Bible he had saved from his home. The kid opened it to the inside cover, his hand shaking. Ollie pointed at a scribble of handwritten text next to the 'Owned By' line. "See? Right there."

Francis dropped this stolen baton. It hit the ground with a puff of dust. There, plain as the day, was his own name—neat as you could be, written in a child's handwriting: *Francis Ellis Hackney.* "You wrote that in."

Even Ollie could tell Francis hadn't meant it. Francis recognized his own scribble. The slanted 'H' in Hackney was unmistakable.

Ollie bit his lip, hiding the split skin in his mouth. He sucked in a deep breath, squeezing the pages. "Dad was really proud of you. He really couldn't stop talking about you to everyone."

Now that was true. It was half the reason Francis offed the old guy in the first place. Sinclair Hackney's bragging about a serial killer son had traveled down the grapevine all the way to Francis' hideaways. It took one newspaper article for Francis to decide the old man needed to go.

Francis glanced at Ollie's nametag, and snatched the Bible from him to take a closer look at the script from a time he had long forgotten after his first taste of arterial spray. "'Blake' is a fake name, I take it?"

"No, that one's real." Ollie rubbed the back of his knuckles, quickly glancing at Coal and Chaplin as they watched on silently. Francis could have cared less what those two morons thought. The kid was his baby brother. He *had* a baby brother. Ollie continued, his voice softer and reminiscent. "It's my Mom's name. Dad never married her, and he really wasn't interested in custody."

Ollie snorted in a way so bitter Francis did a double take. A hardening fell over those green eyes, that opened a door Francis wanted to stay slammed shut. Ollie stared at Francis with eyes that would have been his old man's if they were a shade different. "I was lucky he even acknowledged I was his son at all."

"You ever going to tell me?" Francis snapped the book closed, and threw it at Ollie. He caught it before it could hit the ground, shoving it quickly back in his jacket like Francis would take it from him again without notice. Francis voice cracked. "Or were you just going to keep cuddling up next to me like some wanton whore while keeping this juicy little tidbit to yourself!?"

"I never decided! I just wanted to get to know you first before I came forward, and by that time things were going so well that I didn't want to ruin anything..." Ollie trailed off, staring at the ground again.

"And you wanted to meet the big brother who killed your family, why again?" Francis asked, his voice choked in his throat.

"You're my big brother, the only family I have." Ollie smiled, far too sweetly and far too forgiving. "I had nowhere else to go."

CHAPTER 14

LYLE CHAPLIN DIDN'T believe what Blake said for a heartbeat.

A kid that good looking, that nice, and that smart had nowhere to go but a rotting prison full of the most crazed and deranged inmates the mainland couldn't deal with? Even if he wasn't lying about having no other family than Francis—no, there was something bigger going on. Something behind those green eyes radiated a truth behind that lie. Worse yet, the brother thing was probably true. That worried Lyle far more than the idea Blake had a crush on Francis.

Lyle's hand clenched on the shotgun. Vernon close beside him.

Francis was too far gone in the shock of the boy's revelation to see it. Vernon had hidden too far back in his head to notice anything past his ever running soap opera. Lyle was alone on the 'Blake is probably ten times crazier than we ever thought' front, so he kept his mouth shut. He let his brain keep track, and his finger on the trigger instead. Lyle wouldn't deny though, he wanted to know what Guard Oliver Blake was hiding. Even Shepherd liked the kid, and that man was crazier than the folks in J-Block.

"Francis," Lyle said. He studied the gruff man's face as he turned from Blake. There was an odd twitch in the man's eye that set Lyle's back straight. Francis didn't have all his eggs in a basket either, it paid to remember. Lyle pushed Vernon at the small of his back so the man would start walking as he trembled. "I think we should save this talk for the boat. We're burning moonlight and I don't want to wait for the leftover lunatics to abandon the prison."

"You're right." Francis pressed the back of his hand against Blake's lapels as he walked by. He refused to look at the kid, even has his hand lingered on the Bible hidden under the pressed black fabric. The man's untouched uniform seemed out of place during a prison riot—even his tie was still neatly tucked into the vest underneath. Neither Blake nor Francis said another word to each other, both keeping their eyes elsewhere.

Lyle hoisted the shotgun up in his arms and headed down the hill. Vernon followed, his arms crossed and his eyes jerking around. Lyle pushed him a step forward, and farther away from Francis and Blake. "Let's move."

"Since when were you made the leader of this little group?" Francis asked, but without any bite. He pulled out his ever-present box of cigarettes and flipped open the lid with his thumb. He stopped walking. Lyle waited a few steps ahead, and grabbed Vernon's sleeve to keep the mumbling man from walking too far ahead. Francis patted his pockets down, before dropping his hands to the side. He looked like someone stole a kill out from under him. "I'm outta' smokes."

Blake tapped a plain white box on Francis' shoulder twice. The man jumped reflexively before turning and grabbing the kid's jacket. Blake handed him the box, as if he hadn't noticed he had just been hauled an inch off the ground, and averted his gaze to the grass. He looked like a chastised schoolboy. "I figured you'd go through that last pack faster than usual."

"When did you get that? Was it in your pocket? This whole time?" Vernon asked, pushing by Lyle.

Vernon shuffled from one foot the other, trembling in place. His beady eyes focused between Blake and the box in Francis' hand. His concentration was intense—just how much did he really pay attention? He had a point though—where *did* Blake get the cigarettes? Did he just... carry spare boxes on him at all time in case Francis needed it?

Lyle hugged the gun closer to his chest.

Vernon stomped his foot, in the childish manner he was so fond of parading about. He pointed at Blake, his eyes opening unnaturally wide. "I didn't see you leave to get them."

"You don't see much of anything," Francis said, opening the pack and placing a stick in his mouth. He took a step in front of Blake, blocking Vernon's view. "Just your stories."

"I can see just fine," Vernon huffed. He shuffled back to the side and crossed his arms. He gazed at Blake wearingly. The guard matched his gaze, his eyes re-focusing just enough to avoid being a glare, but still show his annoyance. Blake's 'brother' story just kept gaining ground. Vernon backed into Lyle's side, and grabbed his jacket. "Just fine."

Lyle moved. They needed to get to the boat, and far, far away from all that bad blood.

CHAPTER 15

OLIVER RUBBED HIS eyes under the bill of his hat. His secret was out, and Francis took things as well as Oliver assumed he would. But those worries would have to wait for a later date. Their group of four was currently watching the commotion down below while hidden behind a chest-high stone wall that overlooked the lower docks on a hill. A field of ankle-high wild grass blew softly behind them, dotted here and there with a dandelion. The children's homemade soccer goals stood tall on either end of the field, lonely at night. Oliver taped his fingers on the crumpled grey stone. His bad night was just starting, it looked like.

The inmates who hadn't stayed behind to maim or fight, had gathered before the main boat. He counted about thirty or forty men squabbling like alley cats fighting over scraps.

The ship's captain and crew were slaughtered on the sidewalk. Their bodies strewn about like rag dolls—their innards spilled, and clothes torn. Oliver rested his forehead on the stonewall. What was that little girl going to do when she came by for fishing in the morning? The captain always had a smile on his old face, and a story about his granddaughter. Oliver knew her inside and out, even if he only met her once or twice a year. To see his head split on the rocks—to know that little girl would see—was... nauseating.

Oliver crouched down and took a steadying breath, while down below the inmates argued over how to operate the boat, loud and obnoxious as small children.

Francis leaned on the wall, standing tall and in sight with his legs a few inches from Oliver's shoulder. Smoke drifted from his cigarette, any recommended caution about attracting attention was ignored in the revelation of their shared blood. Oliver crouched against the wall, watching the man who'd consumed most of his thoughts since he was three or four. Francis was everything and nothing like Oliver had come to imagine him. Though he supposed his sources hadn't been all that accurate, even if the information flow was constant.

Dad never stopped talking about his precious Hackney Hacker.

He would get this light in his eye, and this crooked smile on his face that Oliver had seen on Francis nearly every other day. He'd lean on his bar counter, bragging to Mother, or the neighbors. Perfect Francis. The serial killer who was a chip off the old block.

"He's just like me! Save for the killing part," He'd joke with a laugh.

Oliver heard the good and the bad, but was forever curious about this man who was supposedly so much like the one who ignored his other son. Oliver hardly went a day without hearing about his brother. And he always listened to every word Dad was willing to give.

Oliver wanted to meet Francis.

But the one time Francis had come home, Oliver had missed him. It was unfair. His big brother took everything. The least he could do was let Oliver see for himself just how wonderful he was. To see what was so damn special that Oliver's own years of perfect behavior and obedience meant shit.

Oliver sucked in a breath, and gripped his fists. Calm. He was calm. He worked hard for his well behaved demeanor and good cheer, and he wouldn't lose it over this. He'd get past it. Oliver glanced above at the rugged man smoking, biting the corner of his lip.

At least Francis lived up to expectations.

"Don't suppose you know how to drive a ship, Ollie?" Francis asked. He tapped his cigarette on the wall, gesturing vaguely at the inmates below. "'Cause I sure don't, and I doubt those idiots do either. Not a big tugboat like that."

"No," Oliver said.

Francis tapped his cigarette on the wall, spilling the ashes on Oliver's shoulder. They stayed where they fell, in a tiny grey pile. "What about you Chaplin?"

The bulky man adjusted the shotgun on his shoulder. "No."

"So we're stuck? We're stuck. We're stuck!" Coal moaned, holding his head. The man wandered back into the dandelion spotted field. He stumbled one way, and then the other, like a vertical teeter-totter. He gripped his hair, pulling at the black strands like it was his only hold on sanity—eyes were wide as saucers. *Poor guy was losing it*, Oliver thought to himself. Coal mumbled as he paced back and forth, whatever words he had slowly dissolving into gibberish. Oliver knocked the ashes off his shoulder as Coal's chanting turned into white noise. "We're stuck here and the rest of the inmates will be here any minute and then we'll be doomed."

Oliver pulled himself back up to lean against the wall next to Francis. He crossed his arms on the top, staring down at the fight below. Francis and Chaplin studied the lower dock with a sharper eye, looking for their best option, and Oliver let them make the plans for the fighting. He watched the boat, thinking of the times he'd been invited into the captain's area while the man was steering. If they made it past the inmates, perhaps he *could* figure out how to steer the older vessel.

Coal strangled out half a shout before it was smothered into muffled groaning.

Oliver froze in place, as he heard the sound of a twisting squelch; a wet slip of metal and flesh. He inched into a fully standing position, his pulse increasing. A hyena laugh, the tiniest high-pitched giggle, cried out over the thump of a body hitting the dirt and grass.

Francis turned from the wall, steady as a rock. He took a single step in front of Oliver, blocking the view of Coal lying crumpled and bloody in the middle of the field. He wasn't getting back up. Francis pulled the cigarette from his mouth and smashed the lit end into the stone wall. "Liam Hurst."

CHAPTER 16

"WHY DID YOU do that, Liam?" Ollie asked, an odd tightness in his voice. Francis grit his teeth, clenching his fists. If he really, truly shared blood with this kid—who knew what he was hiding under that calm, good-boy Christian facade? Would Ollie start showing his secrets, now that he was cornered by his lies? Would being confronted by the one guard he probably recognized was crazy from day one be enough to release a beast? Ollie shouted, "He wasn't doing anything to you!"

Hurst tapped the edge of his switchblade against his lips, leaving a pucker of blood across his mouth. He licked at the red stain, missing a smudge just under the left of his nose. He giggled. "He was there?"

Chaplin shot Hurst in the chest.

The buckshot littered the front of his jacket, burnt with soot. Hurst stumbled back grabbing at his shirt, his eyes wild. Francis shoved Ollie against the wall, when Chaplin snapped the barrel down to reload. His eyes were wet, and the snarl that came from his mouth was inhuman with rage. The gentle giant was dead, and this one was screaming for Jack's head for his bread. Chaplin clapped the barrel of the weapon back into place, lifting the shotgun to blow that psycho's head off.

His target was missing.

Chaplin swung the rifle to smack it into the swift moving figure of Hurst diving into his side, too close for a shot. The ruined front of his shirt revealed the bulletproof vest underneath. Pocks marked his face and neck where the stray buckshot ripped into his skin. Lines of red dripped through the grey. Hurst wasn't to be deterred by pain, though, swinging his knife forward and slashing wildly.

Ollie moved. Francis stopped him. He'd seen this dog-and-pony show before—and not here, not now. Not with a loaded shotgun, a madman and a knife swinging about. Francis had answers he still needed. Answers he'd never known he'd wanted before. Francis felt a lump catch in the base of his throat. Lies or not it was still *Ollie*. He used his entire arm to cover Ollie's shoulder in his distraction and tackled the kid to the ground. He held the boy down, face and stomach deep in the grass while Chaplin and Hurst duked it out above them. The mixed series of shouts and laughter was deafening.

Hurst ducked and weaved like the animal he was, giggling hysterically like he'd just heard his favorite joke. Chaplin, stoic as a rock, alternated between trying to smack him with the rifle butt, and aiming it at the little weasel.

Francis jerked as Ollie struggled to get up. "Let me help, Francis!"

"Nah, we're staying out of this one, kid," Francis said, his hand firmly on the base of Ollie's neck and his knee in the small of the kid's back. He kept the boy facing away from the action, but kept a close eye on where that shotgun was pointing. His free hand was gripped securely around the kid's arm in case he'd have to pull back and roll.

Ollie repaid Francis' concern by elbowing him in the gut as hard as the little brat was able. Francis wheezed as he caught his breath, and Ollie scrambled up. He could practically feel the bruise sprouting and spreading like wild moss. Francis returned fire. He yanked the kid up by his collar, and smashed the kid's head into the ground with an startling crack. He'd live. While Ollie groaned, Francis turned back to the action.

He looked up in time to see a trigger pulled and a knife hit home.

Liam Hurst found himself without a face, and his body gurgling blood from the gaping holes in his neck. The body twitched on the ground for ten seconds before it stilled. Lyle Chaplin collapsed beside him, falling to his knees before toppling over to his side. The gun clattered as it hit the grass. A knife lodged in the side of Chaplin's throat sank an inch deeper upon impact.

Lucky shot for the both of them.

Francis removed himself from Ollie and walked over to Chaplin. He knelt down next to the poor bastard. Chaplin's eyes flickered back and forth in their sockets, eyes still wet over Coal. Francis pulled the knife from his throat as the man gurgled, suffocating. He wiped it and his hands off on the edge of his jacket. Francis sighed, placing the knife in his pocket in the same movement he placed his foot against Chaplin's open neck. He cut off the oxygen flow, as Chaplin tried to swallow. It felt good to have something familiar on his person—this Francis knew how to use.

The shotgun was worthless without ammo, anyway.

Ollie remained on the ground, breathing heavily. His hat lay a few feet away, and he covered his head with his hands. Chaplin stilled after a full minute, from suffocation or blood loss—Francis didn't care to figure out which. He shoved his hands in his pockets as he walked away, his heart picking up the tempo and his insides warm. Francis hauled Ollie to his feet by the kid's elbow, keeping his hands on the trembling figure to hold him upright.

Ollie leaned into him, rubbing his face with his hands as he scrubbed away a fresh track of tears. Ollie didn't seem to have anything to say, and Francis didn't feel much up to conversation either. Not with three freshly dead and beginning to rot with such a sweet smell—Francis squeezed Ollie's shoulders and dropped his forehead into the crook of Ollie's neck. Chaplin and Coal were *friends*. Not toys. *Not toys.* Francis giggled. He shouldn't be getting excited that their excursion was down to two.

"Inmate Francis Ellis Hackney!" Shepherd shrieked, his voice unmistakable behind Francis. "You will return Guard Oliver Blake to me this very instant!"

Francis detached himself from Ollie, and slouched against the wall. He smirked at Shepherd, and popped another cigarette in his mouth. He jerked when it was Ollie who lit the tip with a lighter pulled from nowhere. Francis took in a drag of smoke.

Make that down to three.

CHAPTER 17

EMMANUEL ENJOYED THE hours after dark. The night air was cool around him, and the harsh rays of the sun were tucked away until morning. He did not need the night to hide him, but he vastly preferred its dulcet conditions. It made for pleasant collecting.

He brushed a slight of dirt off his sleeve cuff, and continued down the dirt path toward the staff gathering areas. After a brief interrogation of the ruffians still hanging around the cafeteria, Emmanuel found that his Oliver had been carried off toward the guard's townhouses by Inmate Francis Ellis Hackney, accompanied with his miniature gang. He smoothed a strand of hair back in place with the rest with the side of his thumb. Emmanuel really should have known that would be the reality of it all.

Oliver was so easily influenced. Naive.

But that will be remedied soon enough, Emmanuel mused. After seeing the destruction of the townhouses and Oliver's missing shotgun, it was easy enough to put together where they were headed. Who wouldn't make a break for it on the only boat on the island after ransacking the spoils of the guards' keep? Thankfully the dock wasn't far, because Emmanuel intended to take care of *all* of the ruffians and the trash once he retrieved his Oliver.

Every single shattered teacup would be *avenged*.

As he reached the children's soccer field in the center of their community park, Emmanuel slowed his pace. Down below on the hill he could smell it—blood and powder. Iron and smoke, both bitter and intoxicating with every breath. The wind carried it gracefully. Emmanuel barely spotted Hurst's limp body alongside two lumps in the dark night, before he saw it:

Inmate Francis Ellis Hackney *embracing* his Oliver. *His Guard Oliver Blake.* Emmanuel's fists tightened, and his teeth ground in his mouth. Emmanuel felt his serenity give way to brutality. He chipped a tooth. He saw red.

"Inmate Francis Ellis Hackney!" Shepherd shrieked, the mangling of his voice an affront to his own ears deep beneath the rage. "You will return Guard Oliver Blake to me this very instant!"

The two turned to watch him, a wariness in both of their eyes. Emmanuel stood proud, nonetheless, coated in the blood of those who opposed order—his order. Inmate Francis Ellis Hackney's eyes wandered over the red, drinking it in like scum fondling women in a brothel. Emmanuel was above such things. He was Guard Emmanuel Shepherd. *Guard Emmanuel Shepherd.* Blood was merely the side-effect of art, not some intoxicating drug to ruin one's senses.

But those were topics for another day over coffee and sweets in delicate china cups.

Emmanuel straightened the rose in his lapel, striding forward in smooth, graceful steps. He stepped over the dead bodies, careful not to get their filth on his shoes. The center of his attention huddled together a mere twenty feet away. Emmanuel gripped the closed knife in his palm, his fingers itching to flip the blade out and jab it in Inmate Francis Ellis Hackney's eye.

Then maybe the fool would learn to stop his gaze from going where it shouldn't.

Guard Oliver Blake stood flush with Inmate Francis Ellis Hackney, settled under the degenerate's arm. He was a little lost lamb bleating for someone to save him. Nicotine coated hands clutched Guard Oliver Blake's clean uniform, sullying it with an essence of filth and yellowed soot. Ten feet away, Inmate Francis Ellis Hackney took a step in front of the dear boy. He pushed Guard Oliver Blake him behind like *he* was some sort of guardian. Guard Oliver Blake smacked into the wall, pinned in place by Inmate Francis Ellis Hackney's broad back.

Emmanuel stopped an inch from bumping noses with Inmate Francis Ellis Hackney. Their breath intermingled, stale and rancid. Emmanuel clicked open his knife, letting it hang at his side. A warning more so than an immediate threat. He didn't want to start a fight this close to Guard Oliver Blake. Emmanuel had no desire to see the boy hurt in any crossfire. Any confrontation between him and the repulsive, uncouth Inmate Francis Ellis Hackney was sure to be…involved.

Emmanuel pictured Earl Grey and rose print. He smiled pleasantly, sugaring his voice. "Return Guard Oliver Blake to me."

"Sorry, can't do that." Inmate Francis Ellis Hackney shoved his hands into his pocket. He could see the man's garish hands circle around something. Emmanuel watched for the grand appearance of Francis Ellis Hackney's own weapon. The inmate grinned a crooked grin, yellow stained teeth wide and smiling. "If anyone's going to kill him, it'll be me."

CHAPTER 18

OLIVER'S HEART LURCHED into his throat like that swallow of medicine that refuses to go down. Francis' words stung his ears and jabbed like a knife wound in his belly. That wasn't supposed to happen. Oliver was supposed to be special! He gripped Francis' jacket, still trapped between his friend and the stone wall. "What?"

Francis ignored him, a trait he should not have shared with their father. Instead of answering Oliver, Francis whipped his knife out of his slacks pocket. The blade was under Em's chin before anyone could blink. It glistened, the sharp edge reflecting the light as if to show off its dangerous intentions, but Em didn't so much as flinch. Oliver tensed, feeling like a lamb caught between two wolves.

Francis grinned wide, revealing his canines in his best impression of a predator. "Come on, Shepherd. Don't play that good guy routine.

"I can see it in your eyes, you know. This is your big chance to get the kid alone to slit his throat, or whatever it is you do."

"Don't be absurd, and stop projecting your own degenerate desires on me." Em lifted his own knife, clicking the two blades together. He pushed Francis' knife aside with the edge of his, as delicately one would push aside an offered tea cup. Em looked more offended than threatened. "I am merely rounding up my men together for safety. Guard Oliver Blake is one of *my* men, and I will not let you take him to do with as you please."

"You're still going to pull that polite act? A killer knows a killer, *Em,* and if you don't end up slaughtering every last one of your precious guards by morning, I'm a horse's uncle." Francis jabbed his arm forward into Em's chest. He crushed the rose on his lapel, sending the man stumbling over Lyle's unmoving body. Em dropped his knife in the fall, and turned to grab it. "And last I checked, my brother didn't have kids."

Francis was on Em faster than a rabid dog. He punched the head guard across the face, before digging his blade into the prone man's waist at the belt line. It had been so quick, Oliver would have missed it if he blinked. It was the handiwork of someone who knew their skill set inside and out. Easy as breathing. Oliver stood still, leaning on the rock wall for support while Em snarled like a rabid dog, grabbing Francis' loose hair and yanking himself forward to head-butt Francis. Their skulls cracked together, and Oliver's knees locked. His breath grew irregular and painful in his chest.

Is this shock?

Francis backhanded Em across the cheek, knuckles connecting with teeth. He straddled the guard, digging the knife deeper, just under the protective vest and into the soft flesh. Francis' hand was thick with the blood pooling around the two in the grass. "And like I said, I got dibs."

Em snaked his hands around the handle of Francis' knife, keeping it from moving any deeper or across. Francis chuckled, sucking a taste of red from the side of his thumb.

"Why on earth would you want to kill him?" Em asked between gasps, as Francis needled the weapon back and forth in the slick flesh. Em smiled, blood between his teeth. "Isn't he your little favorite?"

"He's also my little brother, if you'd believe it. Found that out for myself today, in fact," Francis said, the promise of madness echoing in his cheerful conversation. Oliver groped for the back wall behind him as his knees buckled. That was one tone he *hadn't* ever heard from his father. Francis leaned over to meet Em face to face. "And since I killed the rest of my family with my own two hands, that means I've got dibs, don't you think? If anyone else killed him, I'd look sloppy!"

"Nonsense," Em spit out. He maintained his dignity somehow while bleeding from the gut. The way he sounded, Em could have been supping tea in his living room while discussing the latest play to enter the mainland theatre. Oliver's stomach twisted, and the gurgling nausea only increased as Em's face shifted into a wicked grin, a high contrast to his classy tone. "Sloppy is the kill of that German fellow that got you caught."

Oliver flinched.

Francis yanked the knife from its hold on Em's waist. He stabbed it into the side of Em's neck with a vitriol that belonged in a horror novel, gracing Em with a matching wound to his friend, Lyle Chaplin.

Heavy breathing filled the air, a sound loud among the insects crawling in the grass. Oliver held onto the wall, slumped against the stone blocks. He felt hot and humid in the cool night air, scared to move while Francis kept his hands plastered to the knife, holding it in place until Em's twitching body stopped moving. Blood covered Francis' hands, mixing with the leftovers of Chaplin.

Em was dead. Oliver couldn't breathe.

Francis rubbed his hand on his pants, before getting his knife back. He used his foot on Em's chest to brace as he yanked the silver weapon free. The resulting kick rolled the guard's head to face Oliver. Francis walked away, wiping the blade on his pants with a click of his tongue. He searched for his pack of cigarettes in his pockets, and not finding them, he searched the ground. Oliver's breath hitched. Em's eyes stared dead out into the field, flower petals littered on his uniform from the shattered rose.

CHAPTER 19

FRANCIS WONDERED IF the kid was broken, as he snatched his pack of cigarettes from the grass. Ollie wasn't doing too hot, hyperventilating and eyes open wider than Coal's after he got a little sneak of something good. Francis nudged Ollie's knee with his foot, while scratching the back of his neck. He was either upset about Shepherd being dead, or that Francis threatened to kill him. He hoped it was the latter as he lit a cigarette. "You know that 'I got dibs' thing was more of a, 'nobody gets to touch him but me' thing than a 'I'm gonna kill that kid first,' thing— right?"

The kid's response made Francis realize it looked like it was the former.

Ollie crawled over to Shepherd, looping his arms around the dead man's chest. He dragged the body away from Coal and Chaplin to lay Shepherd on his back. The kid took care shifting the head so it stared upwards at the dark sky. Francis spit out his cigarette, and stomped it out in the grass. The ashes sizzled under his toe as the kid's hand lingered over the Shepherd's eyes, moving to close the lids. Ollie stopped an inch from the lashes, and left the eyes open. Instead, he positioned Shepherd's arms at the sides, hands crossed at the waist. Ollie fixed the blood soaked flower back into place on the lapel, and spread the loose petals around over Shepherd's hair.

Then he got on his damned knees, and knelt his head in *prayer*.

Francis lit another cigarette.

"Don't tell me you actually liked that psycho?" Francis asked. Ollie knelt his head lower, and his face scrunched up in irritation. Francis yanked his cigarette from his mouth and threw it in the grass. Another wasted stick. His fists tightened, blood squelching in the wrinkles. "He was just using you, kid."

"No, he wasn't. I know that Em cared about me, even if it was in his own crazy way," Ollie said, looking up. His eyes were glossed, and his cheeks wet—but the look behind them was fierce. Francis shoved his hands in his pocket. He had to look away. Ollie stood and brushed the dirt from his knees, before delivering his sucker punch. "Just like you do."

"And if I change my mind about that?" Francis asked. "I'm still pretty miffed about you lying to me, Ollie."

"I'm not dead, yet," Ollie said, simple as that. Like saying the sky is blue, or dead grass is yellow. "You've been throwing yourself in front of me since the lights went out. If that doesn't say you care, I don't know what does. I doubt finding out I'm your brother would change that."

Francis snorted, cuffing the boy on the side of Ollie's temple with his knuckles. He smeared the tan skin with Shepherd's blood, dragging it down the temple. The red looked good on Ollie. The dripping streak molded to the shape of Ollie's cheek, a few droplets landing on his clean pressed jacket. "I killed your folks, you know."

Ollie's gaze didn't wave for an instant. "Aren't we supposed to be fighting for the boat?"

"Kid, we ain't getting on that boat, so let's have that chat. I killed your folks." Francis held the knife under Ollie's neck, an odd case of déjà vu.

The same rush. The same rapid heartbeat. The same defiant glare.

"And years before that I killed my mom, too. My entire family outside of you has died by my knife." Francis cut a slight sliver in the boy's neck. They both shivered. "And I do hate being sloppy."

CHAPTER 20

OLIVER SAW IT. The shift of focus in Francis eyes—the glazed, trance state Oliver remembered from the yard when the B-Block inmate was murdered and started it all. The same look he got tackling Em. The same look he likely had killing their father. The eyes of a killer. A murderer. Hacker Hackney. Daddy's favorite.

His big brother.

The chilled metal brushed Oliver's neck, slitting the skin open in a thin red line.

Oliver hugged Francis.

Warm blood slid under his collar, staining the white shirt and dripping against Oliver's skin. The self-inflicted wound stung, but it was merely a scratch. Nothing Oliver couldn't handle as he tightened his arms around his big brother. He buried his nose in Francis' chest, inhaling the aged smoke. Oliver knew this smell better than he knew himself. The smell of smoke. It belonged to Oliver. He was the one who kept bringing Francis cigarettes. The man would never smell of this without Oliver. Francis owned that scent, but it was Oliver who paid for it.

And Oliver hadn't come all this way for nothing.

Hadn't put up with being second best his entire damned life to be ignored now.

Francis stiffened. Oliver could hear the choked sound he made through his ribcage. Francis' fallen cigarette sizzled in the grass. The smoke wafted up in streams of white ribbon. Oliver twisted his fingers in the back of Francis' worn button-up, squeezing him tighter.

"This is where I'm supposed to be, Francis." Oliver breathed in the smell of soak, sweat and blood. A unique mixture of shame and family.

"So do what you have to."

Francis relaxed, and the knife clattered to the grass. Oliver felt the *thump* of the older man's chin resting on his head. A hand rubbed his back. Francis mumbled into his hair, "You're something else, you know that kid?"

Oliver did now.

CHAPTER 21

THE SUN ROSE over the horizon, and Francis sat side by side with his brother. There were no bars to be found on this stone wall on the hill above the docks. No difference between inmate and guard at all.

Just family.

Ollie had shed his jacket and vest, opting to sit and read the Good Book quietly in the early morning sunlight. A night of quiet understanding rested between them, while Ollie's pistol sat fully loaded and useless on the top of the wall next to Francis' thigh.

Behind them, Chaplin and Coal had been moved to lie side by side. Francis surprised himself by being the one to eventually move them into something less neglectful. Francis supposed he owed them that much. Their eyes were closed, though, unlike Shepherd who still stared into the warming sky.

Chaplin and Coal deserved the rest together.

His friends slept, Ollie read, and Francis did what he did best: Lit another cigarette like the chain smoker he was.

They had always been his biggest weakness.

Who left a cigarette butt at the scene of a murder? Shepherd hadn't been wrong calling that wonderful moment 'sloppy,' Francis would give the dead man that. He sucked in deep, relishing the taste of smoke, and the sight of it curling in the air. It was as beautiful as a blood splatter.

The boat was a bust.

The inmates ran it aground into a rock outcropping after getting it a mere eighteen yards from shore. It sank like a rock when the water filled the main half. Francis had no intention of swimming to shore, and Ollie wasn't exactly up for it either. There was nothing to do but wait for the authorities to notice Tobias Memorial had been toppled.

He had no clue what everyone else had gotten up to that night. Francis blew a puff of smoke, and spoke for the first time since he'd settled Chaplin and Coal. "You think everyone left in the prison is dead?"

"I doubt it," Ollie flipped a page. He pulled his fingers down the page, tracing the words as he read. Ollie must have gotten something from the book that Francis had missed when it was once his. Ollie flipped to the next page. "Someone had to win the fights."

"Good point." Francis flicked the remainder of his cigarette down the hill toward the dock. The stub spun in the air as it traveled, hitting the grass with a slight spark and a burst of ash. Francis hiked a leg up on the wall. "So, what happens now?"

Ollie closed his book with a snap. He picked up his coat and threw it over his shoulder as his feet hit the grass. Ollie's posture was straighter than it'd ever been, and there was a determination he hadn't seen before. Francis hopped off the wall when the kid was halfway down the hill. "Where are you going?"

"The ship captain's daughter was coming at dawn to go fishing," Ollie said, tucking his brother's Bible under his arm. He readjusted his hat on his head, struggling to keep the jacket on his shoulder. "I figure we can catch a ride to shore on her boat, and I fully expect you to keep your hands to yourself."

Francis grabbed the pistol from its spot on the wall, and skipped down the hillside, tumbling after Ollie. The boy had a determined look on his face, searching the shore for the little girl's boat. "What happened to that whole stay here and turn myself in plan? Doesn't this go against your goody-two shoes thing?"

"Are you going to turn yourself in when the authorities arrive?" Ollie answered without even bothering to turn around. His stride was even, and there was a smile on his lips. Fire in his eyes. Where'd all that confidence come from all of a sudden?

"Uh, no." Francis rolled his shoulder back, tapping Ollie's piece against his leg. "I was going to knock out a cop and steal his boat."

"See? I'm saving lives and time by keeping track of you myself." Ollie had the nerve to smirk. He dropped the grin into a more serious smile, sort of sad in a way that reminded Francis of his old man. It was in the pull of the muscle in his cheek. But there was something more. Something even more familiar. "I'm not losing my big brother again."

Francis slapped Ollie between his shoulder blades. "Going on the run then with big brother? You'll be arrested yourself if we get caught you know."

"Yes," Ollie grinned up, green eyes sparkling. He patted Francis' shirt with his hand, rubbing the palm up and down on the fabric. "But I think we can run for a little while. I also fully plan to make sure you behave."

"Not sure how you'll accomplish that, but I'll enjoy watching you try. Behaving myself, can you even picture that?" Francis laughed. He pulled at his sleeve, and listened to his feet crunching in the grass. The sun was above his head, and his brother matched his pace. It was...nicer than it should be. *At least for now*, Francis thought. "I might be able to live with that."

"As long as I keep buying you smokes, you mean?" Ollie had the nerve to hold his nose up.

He ruffled the kid's hair something fierce, dragging him into a headlock. "You got it, kid."

Acknowledgements

To God be the glory forever, and ever, Amen.

As always: Thanks to God in the highest for the talent to write, and the push He gave to everyone who inspired me, helped me, and encouraged me. And of course, thanks be to God for giving us Jesus, who loves you & me.

At this particular moment: Thank you to everyone who took the time to tell me to continue publishing when I wasn't at my best, and when my writing career seemed to come to a stand still before it even really got started. This book would not have made it without everyone, whether friends, family or both, who made sure to keep bugging me to write more.

To keep going, and to not be afraid.

Thank you for every bit of encouragement I've been given from readers like you, as well. Your comments and kind words are so valuable to me.

I appreciate it more than I think I could ever tell you in words.

About The Author

Grey Liliy is a young woman who claims the East Coast of Virginia as her home. She enjoys anime, video games, movies, novels, and comics of just about any genre. Liliy has been drawing & writing a comic of her own since 2005, called *The Adventures of Wiglaf and Mordred,* which you can find at http://liliy.net/wam. Her debut novel, *Children of Hephaestus* was published in September 2012 and is available now.

www.ingramcontent.com/pod-product-compliance
Lightning Source LLC
Chambersburg PA
CBHW071955230626
47052CB00014B/1165